The Author

MORDECAI RICHLER was born in Montreal, Quebec, in 1931. Raised there in the working-class Jewish neighbourhood around St. Urbain Street, he attended Sir George Williams College (now a part of Concordia University). In 1951 he left Canada for Europe, settling in London, England, in 1954. Eighteen years later, he moved back to Montreal.

Novelist and journalist, screenwriter and editor, Richler, one of the most acclaimed writers, spent much of his career chronicling, celebrating, and criticizing the Montreal and the Canada of his youth. Whether the settings of his fiction are St. Urbain Street or European capitals, his major characters never forsake the Montreal world that shaped them. His most frequent voice is that of the satirist, rendering an honest account of his times with care and humour.

Richler's many honours included two Governor General's Awards and innumerable other awards for fiction, journalism, and screenwriting.

Mordecai Richler died in Montreal in 2001.

MORDECAI RICHLER

The Incomparable Atuk

With an Afterword by Peter Gzowski

This book was first published in Canada by
McClelland and Stewart in 1963.
Copyright © 1963 by Mordecai Richler
Afterword copyright © 1989 by Peter Gzowski

This New Canadian Library edition 1989

National Library of Canada Cataloguing in Publication Data

Richler, Mordecai, 1931–2001
The incomparable Atuk

(New Canadian library)
Bibliography: p.
ISBN 0-7710-9973-8

I. Title.   II. Series.

PS8535.I34A92 1989   C813'.54   C89-094602-7
PR9199.3.R5A92 1989

We acknowledge the financial support of the Government of Canada through
the Book Publishing Industry Development Program for our publishing
activities. We further acknowledge the support of the Canada Council for the
Arts and the Ontario Arts Council for our publishing program.

Printed and bound in Canada by Webcom

McClelland & Stewart Ltd.
75 Sherbourne Street
Toronto, Ontario
M5A 2P9
www.mcclelland.com/NCL
5 6 7 8   12 11 10 09

Contents

"What would happen in Canada if full sovereignty were invoked and the southern border were sealed tight against American mass culture – if the air-waves were jammed, if all our comic books were embargoed, if only the purest and most uplifting of American cultural commodities were allowed entry? Native industries would take over, obviously. Cut off from American junk, Canada would have to produce her own."

Richard H. Rovere, *Maclean's*, Nov. 5, 1960

Part 1 What You Dare to Dream, Dare to Do

1

Twentyman's dreadful equipment was unloaded at a dock in Montreal on a cold wet Wednesday. As reporters pressed forward, uniformed security men wheeled the crate into a private railway car that had been held in readiness on a nearby siding. There were in fact many crates, each a different size or shape, all but one empty. A typically cunning Twentyman manœuvre calculated to frustrate the curious, watchful crowd assembled on the dockside. If the manœuvre was typical of Twentyman it was also, as usual, wholly successful. Even Jean-Paul McEwen, the most astute journalist in Canada, couldn't find out what, if anything, was in which crate. She had to return to Toronto empty-handed. Worse. Her chartered aeroplane was ordered to circle the field until another one had landed safely.

'Who in the hell's in that other plane?' McEwen demanded, outraged.

'Some Eskimo. Wait.' The pilot listened in on his radio. 'His name's Atuk '

McEwen lit up another Schimmelpenninck as her plane was obliged to circle the field for a further ten minutes. 'I'm going to remember that name,' she said.

Atuk.

Atuk, the incomparable, came to Toronto from Baffin Bay in 1960. As every Canadian schoolboy now knows it was out there on the tundra that the young Eskimo had been befriended by a Royal Canadian Mounted Policeman who had fed and clothed him and taught him English. At first Sgt Jock Wilson, generous to a fault but no man of letters, had discouraged Atuk from writing poetry. He had pointed out to the lad that verses would not get him the bigger, better igloo he craved and, what's more, his writing was ungrammatical. But when Atuk persisted Sgt Wilson showed his poems around to the fellows at the local trading post. The clerks, as he expected, could not detect even a feeble talent, but a visiting advertising executive, Rory Peel, was impressed. 'It's a gasser,' he said. 'A real gasser.'

The Twentyman Fur Co, a vastly misunderstood enterprise, was, at the time, suffering from a run of foul newspaper publicity and questions in parliament because, it was claimed, the Eskimo was dying of consumption, malnutrition, and even frost-bite, all because of what the white man had done to make his

2

accustomed way of life unfeasible. Peel, the brightest young advertising man in Toronto, was flown north to see if he could come up with an idea. And so, to the everlasting consternation of Sgt Wilson, he gave Atuk two electric blankets, a sack of flour, his cigarette lighter, and twelve bars of chocolate in exchange for a sheaf of his verse. The poems, as everybody knows, later ran in a series of advertisements in magazines all across Canada. A professor from Eglinton University, Norman Gore, sought out Atuk at Baffin Bay, and came back with the ingredients of the now famous volume of poems.

The success of Atuk's book was such that he was flown to Toronto for a literary party at the Park Plaza Hotel. His thoughtful publisher laid in a supply of chocolate bars and put some raw salmon on ice. A press conference was arranged. Atuk was interviewed on television. He was taken to see a midget wrestling match, a striperama, Rabbi Glenn Seigal's Temple, and other wonders of Toronto. Afterwards Atuk simply refused to return to the Bay. Instead he turned to Professor Norman Gore for help.

The front door to Gore's house was ajar and Atuk, following a native practice, walked right in.

'Hallo?'

A scuffle in the living-room. Sounded like a lamp being knocked over. Atuk entered just in time to find Nancy Gore, the professor's nicely plump wife, doing up the top two buttons of her blouse. Her face was flushed.

'Sorry to intrude. I seek the professor.'

A tall, muscular Negro began hastily to dust a table.

'Ah, that will be all, Joseph.'

'Thank you, m'am,' the Negro said; and he fled.

'The professor will be home, ah, shortly . . . if you care to wait. Em, excuse me.'

When Gore turned up an hour later Atuk came right to the point.

'I wish to stay in Toronto,' Atuk said.

'You've had a quick *succès d'éstime*,' Gore said, 'so you think it's easy. Actually, the writer's path in this country is a thorny one.'

'Maybe I will be lucky.'

But Gore was troubled. Though he adored the chunky little primitive, he was not blind to the sly side of his nature. A certain un-Presbyterian shiftiness. It would be enlightening, he thought, to see what might come of a savage innocent in Toronto. No—too cruel.

'Go back to the Bay, Atuk. You will only be corrupted here.'

'No. I stay. Maybe I'll be lucky.'

So Gore, although still apprehensive, sent Atuk to see Harry Snipes.

Harry Snipes was a protégé of Buck Twentyman's. Always interested in *kitsch*, he had recently accepted the editorship of *Metro, the magazine for cool canucks*, and in fact wrote most of that immensely popular journal under such pseudonyms as Hilda Styles (Why Women From Halifax to Vancouver Menstruate Monthly), Hank Steele, Jr (I Married An Intellectual Cockroach in Calgary), Sir Horace Simcoe-Taylor, Our Correspondent to the Royal Court (Tony – Lucky Chump or Plucky Champ), and so forth.

Atuk was shown into Snipes's office.

'Well, well, lemme see,' Snipes consulted a typewritten sheet on his desk. 'Uh-huh . . . mm . . . Gore says you're quite a poet.'

Atuk lowered his eyes modestly.

'Well, I've read your stuff, old chap. It's Georgian. Cornpoke.' Snipes reached quickly into his desk, brought out a copy of his own most recent book of poems, *Ejaculations, Epiphanies, et etc*, signed it, and handed it to Atuk. 'You want to get with it. You want to make your poetry more gutsy.'

Atuk promised he would try.

'That'll be three seventy-five, please.'

Atuk paid up immediately.

'Good. Now lemme see . . . Are you familiar with the *Metro* image?'

'Yes.'

'We're fighting for our life here. We stand for a Canadian national identity and the American mags are trying to drive us out of business. Like fiction?'

'Yes.'

'Good. Now lemme see.' Snipes lifted a copy of the Aug. 4, 1940 issue of *Collier's* off a stack of old magazines and neatly razored out a short story. 'Here's a good one. I want you to re-set it in Moose Jaw 1850. We haven't any Western yarns for the May issue. But please remember to change more than the names. Play around with the physical descriptions and details. Use your imagination, Atuk. That's what we're paying you for.'

If Atuk failed at his first magazine assignment, he did extremely well in his exams at Eglinton Evening College.

'Attention, class. *Moby Dick* is a sea novel by one, Nicholas Monsarrat; two, Herman Melville; three, C. S. Forester.'

All the heads bent dutifully forward; the pencils began to scratch.

'But this is a two-part question.'

A collective moan.

'How would you categorize this novel? One, adventure; two, animal lore; three, symbolical.'

Atuk and the others were allowed a bit more time for that one.

'Next question. Hamlet's girl friend was called, one, Madame Bovary; two, Franny; three, Ophelia.'

After the exam Atuk ran into Professor Gore in the hall. The Professor, obviously enjoying himself immensely, was deep in conversation with a tubby, middle-aged man; he gestured for Atuk to join him. 'You must meet my friend Panofsky,' he said.

Panofsky's smile was radiant with good nature.

'But do continue,' Professor Gore said.

'Well, it's not that I'm an anti-Gentile,' Panofsky said, 'but look at it this way. The greatest Jewish politicos of our age were Trotsky and Ben-Gurion. *Their* apogee. Eisenhower.'

'So what,' Professor Gore said, nudging Atuk.

'Can you imagine them shouting in the Red Square "I Like Leon"?'

Gore had to yield there.

'Or can you see us in the streets of Tel Aviv wearing buttons that say "I Dig Dave"?'

'You're a treasure. A real treasure, Mr Panofsky,' Gore said. Once Panofsky had excused himself, Gore turned to Atuk. 'That fellow gives me more pleasure . . .' Gore linked arms with Atuk. 'This Panofsky, you know, is one of our more promising sociology students. He's been collecting data for years for a paper on heredity and environment in Protestant society. Oh, but I keep forgetting. You know his son.'

'Do I?'

'Rory Peel. The very fellow who brought your first poems out of the North.'

2

Bad day. Rory Peel's life was ordered by omens and he had only been up briefly when he realized that all the signs were negative. Twentyman Communications down a point and a quarter. Kosher Beef-Frye burnt. His father wanted to see him. Constipation. First licence plate he saw ended with an odd number. Then Michele summoned him back to the kitchen and handed him the foul-smelling parcel.

'Oh – sorry – forgot.'

The day at the office, clouded by the duty to be done, had been a waste. He had been unnecessarily rude to Miss Stainsby and he could have been more enthusiastic on the phone with Snipes. Yet getting drunk won't help, he thought. In the end I'm going to have to take the parcel, walk in there alone in front of all those people, and return it. Rory called for the waiter. 'Another Scotch. A double.'

'Yes, sir, Mr Peel. Right away.'

Rory Peel lived in an enormous ranch-style house overlooking the ravine with his wife, Michele, and three plump, well-adjusted children: Neil, Valery, and Garth.

There was a sun-roof above the house and a pool in the garden below. Music by Muzak filled all the rooms with restful sounds. The toilet and the garage, the bedrooms, the kitchen and the playrooms, were all connected by an intercom system. A bodiless voice generally commanded callers to identify themselves. All lighting was indirect and all heating automatically regulated. Five television sets could be operated by remote control. No air entered the house without having been filtered for germs. Everybody and everything in the house, including domestics, callers, delivery boys and guests, were insured, according to individual need, against death, accidents, fire, polio, acts of God, theft, inability to work through illness, rain on holidays and fall-out: even Garth, who was only seven, subscribed to a retirement plan.

We have so very, very much to be grateful for, Rory thought. When I think how far I've risen above my father. In only one generation from cringing greenhorns in the slums to a relaxed, secure life in the suburbs. Amazing. Only in Canada, he thought. *I ought to leave the bar right now.* But the offensive parcel was still lying in wait in the trunk of the car. I'll bet I could dump it in a field without being caught. No; *she'd* find out.

'I see no reason in the world,' Michele said, 'why you can't take it back.'

'Must we make a fuss? You know what people are.'

The bar bill came to eight-fifty. Rory signed it. Outside the supermarket he smoked three cigarettes in his car before he opened the trunk, got the parcel out, and walked right into the store and asked for the manager.

Mr Toby smiled.

'My name's Peel,' Rory muttered, his heart thumping, 'I'm Jewish.'

'Why some of our best customers are Jews.'

'Oh, yes, certainly. How good of you – it's this roast – my wife, yesterday – look I don't want to make a fuss – not fresh – it's not that I really want the money back, I'm not that kind of a – of a—'

'But it's no trouble at all.'

Mr Toby, still smiling, made out a refund slip.

'Why this is just wonderful of you,' Rory said.

'You tell your little lady how sorry we are. It won't happen again.'

'I want you to know,' Rory said, clutching Mr Toby's sleeve, 'that as long as I live, this is *my* supermarket. *I buy here.*'

Rory, to prove his point, grabbed a carriage and began to load up. He felt wonderfully exhilarated. Grateful. Then suddenly his heart began to pound again. A fat dimpled lady picked up a box of strawberries, deviously sprinkled some of its contents over another box, and then placed the overflowing box in her carriage. Wouldn't you know, Rory thought, that she'd be one of ours. He quickly filled two carriages, and as he wheeled over to the cash register – pushing one, pulling the other – he was overjoyed to see that he was going to be checked out by Mr Toby himself. 'Hi,' Rory said.

'Wow! You must have an awful lot of mouths to feed, mister.'

'You think I bought too much?' Rory asked, his voice failing.

'Not for me to say, is it?'

Rory kept his eyes lowered as a boy loaded eight cartons of foodstuffs into the trunk of his car. What am I going to do with it all, he thought. I know; I'll send it to my father's place. For Leo. Anyway, Michele ought to be pleased. I stood right up to that anti-Semite.

But Michele was distressed. 'Mr Twentyman's office phoned. They want you to call back immediately.'

'Oh.'

'Something to do with the . . . equipment.'

'He's just going too far. He's really overstepping the mark this time.'

'But what's it all about?'

'We're not even allowed to discuss it with our wives. Sorry.'

Michele made a face. All right for you, Mr Spite.

3

Atuk's landlady was waiting for him in the hall. 'Your luscious lady friend phoned,' she said.

Atuk called Bette immediately.

'Oh, Atuk dear, I don't want you to force it. I know it's bad for you. Mentally,' Bette said quickly. 'But I thought I might be able to help you tonight.'

'I see,' he said, his voice faltering.

'You must keep at it, Atuk, if you're going to succeed regularly.'

'You are right. But—'

'No buts. Remember what Dr Parks said. *What you dare to dream*,' Bette said, '*dare to do*.'

Atuk cleared his throat and spoke with a sudden and surprising grimness. 'OK. I'll try.'

'See you at eight, then.'

Bette Dolan was Canada's Darling.

She was not the biggest TV star in the country, our only beauty queen or foremost swimmer; neither was she the first Canadian girl to make a film. But Bette Dolan, while in the same tradition as such diverse Canadian talents as, say, Deanna Durbin, Marilyn Bell, Barbara Ann Scott, and Joyce Davidson, surpassed all of them in appeal. Bette Dolan was a legendary figure. A Canadian heroine.

Bette's beginnings were humble. She came from a small town in southern Ontario, the neighbourly sort of place where retired people live. Her fierce father, Gord Dolan, was a body-building enthusiast, a devotee of the teachings of Doc Burt Parks. Once Mr Best Developed Biceps of Eastern Canada he still retained the title of Mr Niagara Fruit Belt Sr. His wife, May, was a long thin woman with a severe mouth. Formerly a school teacher, she was still active in the church choir. The Dolans would have ended their days predictably; he, enjoying an afternoon of manly gossip in the barbers and his sessions in the gym; and she, planning the next meeting of the Supper-of-the-Month Club, if only their surprisingly lovely daughter had not lifted them out of decent obscurity with one superhuman stroke.

Bette Dolan was the first woman to swim Lake Ontario in less than twenty hours.

As if that weren't sufficiently remarkable, she was only eighteen at the time, an amateur, and she beat three others, all professionals, while she was at it: an American, an Egyptian, and a celebrated Australian marathon swimmer. The American and the Egyptian woman gave up early on and even the much heralded Australian was pulled out of the lake and rushed to the hospital after only fourteen hours in the black icy water. But the incredibly young, luscious, then unknown Canadian girl, coached by her own father, swam on and on and on. True, she had sobbed, puked, and pleaded to be pulled out of the water, but, the very first time that happened, Gord Dolan, ever-watchful in the launch ahead, spurred his daughter on by holding up a blackboard on which he had written,

DADDY DON'T LIKE QUITTERS

The young girl's effort in the face of seemingly

13

invincible odds caught the imagination of Toronto as nothing had before. It's true the much-admired Marilyn Bell had already swum the lake, but it had taken *her* twenty hours and fifty-one minutes, and it was much as if her accomplishment, remarkable as it was, redoubled interest in Bette Dolan's attempt to better it. Anyway, the fact is that by six o'clock in the morning a crowd, maybe the largest, certainly the most enthusiastic, ever known in the history of Toronto, had gathered on the opposite shore to wait for Bette. They lit bonfires and sang hymns and cheered each half mile gained by the girl. Television technicians set up searchlights and cameras. Motor-cycle policemen and finally an ambulance arrived.

Back in Toronto, as morning came and radio and television newscasters spoke feverishly of twelve-foot waves, some people prayed, others hastily organized office pools or phoned their bookies, and still more leaped into their cars and added to the largest known traffic jam in Toronto's history. Sunny Jim Woodcock, The People's Prayer For Mayor, spoke on Station CKTO. 'I told you when I was elected that I would put Toronto on the map. Bette Dolan is setting an example here for youth all over the free world. *More power to your elbows, kid!*' The *Standard*, never a newspaper to be caught off the mark, printed two sets of their late morning edition. One with a headline, SHE MAKES IT! WOW!, the other, TOUGH LUCK, SWEETHEART!

On the launch, Gord Dolan watched anxiously, he prayed, kissed his rabbit's foot, and spat twice over his left shoulder, as his daughter struggled against the oncoming waves.

'Please pull me in,' she called. 'Please . . . I can't make it . . .'

He scrawled something hurriedly on the blackboard and held it up for Bette to see again.

THE OTHER BROADS HAVE QUIT. PARK AVE. SWIMWEAR OFFERS $2,500, IF YOU FINISH. DON'T DROWN NOW. DADDY

But Bette had already been in the lake for sixteen hours. The plucky girl had come thirty-four miles. Thrashing about groggily, her eyes glazed, she began to weep. '. . . can't feel my legs any more . . . can't . . . think . . . going to drown . . .'

'All right,' Dolan said, gesturing his girl towards the launch, 'we'll pull you in now, kid.'

But as Bette, making an enormous effort, swam to within inches of the launch Gord Dolan pulled ahead a few more yards.

'Come on, honey. Come to Daddy.'

Again she started for the launch and again Gord Dolan pulled away. 'You see,' he shouted to her. 'You can do it.'

(When Gord Dolan spoke on television several weeks later, after accepting the Canadian-Father-of-the-Year Award, he said, 'That was the psychology-bit. I've made a study of people, you know.')

Initially, the prize money being offered was five thousand dollars, but once the last of the foreign competitors pulled out, as soon as it became obvious that Toronto had taken the surviving Canadian youngster to its heart and, what's more, that she was on the brink of collapse, Buck Twentyman made a phone call. Minutes later a helicopter idled over Gord Dolan's battered launch, a uniformed man descended a rope ladder, and Dolan was able to chalk up on his board,

TWENTYMAN HISSELF OFFERS TEN MORE GRAND — IF YOU MAKE IT. DADDY IS MIGHTY PROUD. GO, BABY.

When Bette Dolan finally stumbled ashore at seven p.m., after nineteen hours and forty-two minutes in the lake, she was greeted by a frenzied crowd. Newsreel cameramen, reporters, advertising agents, some who had prayed and others who had won bets at long odds, swarmed around her. Souvenir-crazed teenagers pulled eels off Bette's thighs and back. The youngster collapsed and was carried off to a waiting ambulance. When she woke the next afternoon it was to discover that her life had been irredeemably altered. Bette Dolan was a national heroine.

As was to be expected, she was immediately inundated with offers to endorse bathing suits, health foods, beauty lotions, chocolate bars, and so forth, but Bette turned down everything. 'I did not swim the lake for personal gain,' she told reporters. 'I wanted to show the world what a Canadian girl could do.'

SHE SWAM THE LAKE — BECAUSE IT WAS THERE, was the title of Jean-Paul McEwen's prize-winning column. Seymour Bone's approach, in his column on the next page, was considerably more intellectual. Quoting Frazer, Jung, Hemingway, and himself from a previous column, he elaborated on man's historical-psychological need to best nature. While he was able to accept Bette as a symbol, Bone reserved judgement on the girl and her motives. He needn't have bothered. The rest is part of the Dolan legend. Surely everybody now knows how she turned the bulk of her prize money over to her town council to build a fantastically well-equipped gym as a challenge to the crippled children; how the Red Feather, the United Appeal, the White Cane, and innumerable other worthy organizations all profited from Bette's television, film, and public appearances. Bette Dolan was incorruptible.

Harry Snipes wrote in *Metro*, The Girl With All The Curves Has No Angles.

She has a heart, Jean-Paul McEwen observed in her column, bigger than Alberta.

Bette was also lovely, unspoilt, radiant, and the most sought-after public personage in the dominion. In earlier times she would have come forth to bless churches, but in Canada, things being what they were, she pulled the switch on new power projects and opened shopping centres here, there, and everywhere.

Wherever Bette went she was instantly recognized. Ordinary people felt better just for having seen her. But if Canada loved Bette Dolan it was also true that she so loved the country that she felt it would be unfair, sort of favouritism, for her to give herself to any one man. So although many, including cabinet ministers, actors, millionaires, and playboys, had tried, Bette remained, in her mother's words, a clean girl. Until, that is, she met Atuk.

Bette first met Atuk at the party for him at the Park Plaza Hotel and saw him again at another party a couple of months later. Atuk was enthralled and promptly asked if he could meet Bette again. To his amazement, she said yes. Actually, Bette was more grateful than he knew because, by this time, nobody bothered to ask her for a date any more. Bette made dinner for Atuk at her apartment. Carrot juice, followed by herb soup and raw horse steak with boiled wild rice. Atuk, thoughtful as ever, had scraped together some money and brought along a bottle of gin. Bette, lithe and relaxed in her leotards, told Atuk about her father and how his life had been changed by the teachings of Doc Burt Parks. She sensed Atuk felt depressed, maybe even defeated by Toronto, and tried her best to encourage him. 'You'll be a success here yet,' she said.

'I don't know. It is so difficult.'

'But success doesn't depend on the *size* of your brain,' she assured him.

Atuk hastily added some gin to the carrot juice.

'Dr Parks has always said,' Bette continued, too absorbed to protest, 'that if you want to succeed you must always shoot for the bull's-eye.'

Atuk promised to try.

'You're as good as the next fellow. You simply must believe that, Atuk. You see, the most successful men have the same eyes, brain, arms, and legs as you have.'

'I drink now. You too.'

'I'll bet,' she said, narrowing her eyes, 'that you envy some people.'

'Many, many people.'

'*But still more people envy you.*'

'Do they?'

'Sure. Some are bald – you have a head full of hair. Some are blind – you can see. *Everybody envies somebody else.* You must learn to have faith in yourself.'

Soon they were sipping gin and carrot juice together nightly and Bette continued to do her utmost to fill Atuk with confidence.

'Why go to so much trouble?' he once asked her.

'Because I have to help people. That's me.' Her long, powerful, Lloyd-insured legs curled under her on the sofa, a lock of blonde hair falling over her forehead, Bette smiled and said, 'Do you realize you're just about the only male who has never – never tried the funny stuff with me?'

'Don't you admire me for it?' he asked hopefully.

'Yes. Certainly I do.' She got down on the floor and began a lightning series of chin-ups. A sure sign she was troubled. 'But don't you love me?' She rolled over on her back, supporting her buttocks with her hands and revolving her legs swiftly. 'Everybody loves Bette Dolan,' she insisted.

'And so do I. Oh, so do I!'

So Atuk told her his dreadful secret. 'I lack confidence,' he said, 'because I am unable to make love. All that stands between me and hitting the bull's-eye is a woman who can . . . well, encourage me over the hump.' He lowered his head. 'I need help, Miss Dolan.'

A plea for help was something Bette Dolan had never taken lightly. She sprang to her feet, bouncing upright. Her lovely face filled with determination. After a long and solemn pause, she said, 'I will help you, Atuk.'

'Would you? Honest?'

To prove it she stepped right up to him, her eyes squeezed shut against anticipated distaste, and kissed him on the mouth. 'It's the very first time for me,' she said.

'I'm so afraid,' Atuk said, his voice quavering, 'of failing.'

Bette kissed him again, forcing his mouth open. When she was done, Atuk cleared his throat and poured himself a rather strong gin and carrot juice.

'Aren't you even . . . don't you feel . . . ?'

'It's no use,' he said.

Bette pulled him down to the rug with her and led his hand to her breast. 'This should be very stimulating for you,' she said. She kissed him even more passionately, rolled over on him, tried a couple of other sure-fire things, and then pulled back to look at him quizzically.

'Well,' he said, 'I do feel a certain . . .'

'Good.'

'I think my pulse-beat *has* quickened.'

'That's progress, isn't it ?'

But it seemed to Atuk there was a sour edge to her voice now.

'That's all for tonight,' she said.

At the door, however, she suddenly clung to him. 'I hope you realize,' she said, 'that no man has ever even held me in his arms before. I couldn't you see. Because I belong to the nation. Like Jasper Park or Niagara Falls.'

'I do understand.'

'I'm trying to help, that's all.'

She had Atuk back early the next afternoon for a lecture.

'I think your trouble may be mental,' she said.

'Very likely. Many times the Old One has said—'

'Well,' she interrupted, taking a deep breath, 'the first thing you must understand is that every human being from the beginning of time has possessed sex organs and was produced as a result of sexual intercourse. Does that shock you?'

Atuk whistled.

'I thought it would. You must learn to think of your sex organ,' she said, drawing a sketch on the blackboard, 'as being just as common as your hands, your heart, or your pectoral muscles. If you analyse the penis as you analyse the function of any other part of your body you will find that it's made up of essentially the same kind of materials.'

'I'm going to love it in Toronto,' Atuk said.

'What?'

'Nothing,' he said, hastily pouring himself another gin and carrot juice.

'Then, to quote Dr Parks, if you analyse the sex act itself in the same clear-thinking way, you will see that this simple function is no more mysterious or filthy than eating, breathing, or urinating.'

After the lecture Bette shed her smock and was revealed in the most provocative silk pyjamas. Her work clothes, she called them off-handedly, and she at once engaged Atuk in a series of practical exercises: therapy. Soon there were lectures every afternoon and by the end of the first week there was rather less time spent at the blackboard and more at therapy. She was, Atuk thought, very inventive for a novice. Usually, she was also the acme of patience. A model teacher. Though there were times when the therapy became so real for her that the final, inevitable disappointment made her petulant.

'I want you,' she ultimately said, 'to go for broke today.'

'You mean shoot for the bull's-eye?'

'Yes,' she said, exasperated. 'I'm not enjoying this, you know. I'm only trying to help. But I'm getting discouraged. You must try to help yourself, you know.'

'I couldn't. I . . .'

Bette sprang up and caught him in a judo hold. 'You shoot for the bull's-eye, goddam it,' she said, 'or I'll . . .'

So Atuk finally made love to Bette.

Afterwards Bette lay so still, she seemed so remote, that Atuk wondered if she suspected that she had been seduced.

But Bette had been lifted into a hitherto unsuspected sphere. It had never occurred to her before that love-making could be anything but nasty. Filthy. Like her father belting her mother into submission in the next room. How utterly wonderful, she thought, that indulging in the funny stuff could be such a generous and Christian thing to do. There was truth, after all, in her mother's saying time and again, that there was no joy greater than helping others.

Atuk spiked his carrot juice with more gin.

'I think,' Bette said, her voice jarringly submissive, 'that you ought to try again, sweetheart.'

And so Canada's Darling, the unobtainable Bette Dolan, became Atuk's grateful mistress, and Atuk was soon reconciled to phone calls at all hours of the day or night.

'You must come over immediately,' she'd say. 'I feel the need to help you.'

So at a quarter to eight Atuk started out of the rooming house, jumped a bus, and hurried over to Bette's place.

Perhaps it was because he was so lonely, maybe he drank too many gin and carrot juices, but that evening Atuk confessed to Bette what he had done on the tundra.

Bette was certainly horrified by the nature of his crime, but she said, 'The case is closed. You have nothing to worry about, darling.'

'I didn't mean any harm. What did I know of such things?'

'Of course, of course,' she said, pulling him to her again.

'You must promise never to repeat what I have told you,' Atuk said, suddenly realizing that he had revealed his most dreadful secret. 'You must swear it, Bette.'

'I swear it. Now come here.'

4

If he didn't go directly to Bette's after his classes at Eglinton, Atuk usually went to the bar around the corner for a bottle of Twentyman's Ale.

A sign outside the bar proclaimed the presence of a rock'n'roll group Direct From the Ed Sullivan Show and a Smash Run in Buffalo, and inside Atuk joined the pale released office workers all bent in a curve over bottles of ale at the horseshoe-shaped bar, a row of pencils still in the breast pockets of their jackets. Over toward the door, a pyramid of rubbers and overshoes lay in a steaming puddle. Atuk felt miserable because it seemed to him that after the initial, hardly profitable, success of his book of poems, he had failed at everything in Toronto except Bette Dolan, but his success with Bette was fraudulent and besides she was too slim for his taste. Oh, he thought, for a fat smelly bear of a girl. Damn. Here he was blessed enough to be in Toronto, and what had he made of himself? Nothing. What had he done for his family? A food parcel. His Tribe? The Elders of the Igloo? Some blurred photographs of strategic bridges, the railway station, the airport. Nothing to shout about. The Old One would be disappointed.

Atuk was bitterly determined to prove to the Old One, Bette, Gore, and Doc Burt Parks, that he was not entirely without vim-and-vigour.

'What you dare to dream,' Dr Parks had said, 'dare to do.'

Bette had introduced Atuk to the great teacher when he had come to Toronto with a group of body-builders. Dr Parks introduced a physical culture display in the sports department of Twentyman's

Department Store, where his equipment was for sale. An enormous crowd had turned up for the exhibition, but this was no surprise, for Bette Dolan had promised to appear.

A magnificently built man of sixty-two, Dr Parks strode masterfully up and down the platform. 'Well, then,' he began, 'I'm sure all you washed-out, weak, worn-out, suffering, sickly men want to renew your youth and delay that trip to the underground bungalow.'

Lake Ontario Jr struck a classic pose.

'We have brought together here some of the finest examples of Canadian manhood in the world. We are building a new race of muscular marvels greater than the Greek Gods. We're doing it for patriotic reasons.'

The Best Developed Biceps of Sunnyside Beach rippled his muscles.

'You too,' Dr Parks told the people, 'can develop a physique like Buddy Lane and overcome constipation, hernia, hardening of the arteries, diarrhœa, impotence, heart disease, and so forth.'

Television cameras dollied in as a nine-year-old French Canadian boy and his father, a man no more than four foot eleven, began a series of amazing exercises.

'This fellow here,' Dr Parks said, 'is the strongest stunted man in the world. *Isn't that something?*'

A few people applauded.

'Body-building is one of the finest means known to man of overcoming juvenile delinquency. If the kid's in the gym you know he's not out getting a fix. Why, I'm sure none of you want your boy to grow up a skinny runt . . . puny! . . . you want him to be a real Parks he-man!'

Next the drums rolled, the cameras came closer, and a big muscular Negro was led onstage. He wore dark glasses.

'Isn't this fellow *something*?' Dr Parks asked.

But the applause was mild, grudging. Atuk was puzzled. He felt sure he had seen the Negro somewhere before.

'Know what he needs,' somebody said, 'a brassière!'

Unperturbed by his luke-warm reception, the black shiny giant lifted a huge weight. Dr Parks whistled with amazement. '*Isn't he* . . . SENSATIONAL?' Dr Parks demanded, beginning to applaud.

'Aw.'

'Where's Bette Dolan?'

'We came to see Bette.'

Dr Parks turned accusingly on his audience. 'You see what he's just done?' he said. He paused. 'Well, *he's blind*!'

The audience gasped. Touched and shamed.

'Meet Jersey Joe Marchette. THE WORLD'S BEST DEVELOPED . . . BLIND . . . NEGRO!'

Now the applause was deafening.

'Like I play the piano too,' Marchette said, grinning.

'Just look at those muscles,' Dr Parks said. 'If he can do it – so can you!'

Jersey Joe Marchette struck another pose.

'Recognize him?' Dr Parks asked.

'Isn't he the guy in the Ever-Black Shoe Spray Commercial?'

'Wrong!'

'He's Mr Klean-All on the Derm Gabbard Show.'

'Wrong again. Tell 'em, Joe.'

'In the Twentyman Steel Four Freedom spots,' Joe said, extremely pleased, 'I'm one of the guys in Freedom From Fear. You know, the guy with the lunch pail and the big smile. There's me and this kike and—'

'OK,' Dr Parks said, 'OK. A big hand for Jersey Joe, folks!'

Marchette was applauded even more wildly this time, but he wouldn't leave the stage. Dr Parks glared at him.

'One minute,' the compère said, rushing onstage. 'We have a special surprise for you, Dr Parks.'

'Oh.'

The compère handed Jersey Joe a big brass plaque.

'Almost forgot,' Jersey Joe said. He wet his lips. 'Dr Parks,' he began, 'I have been asked by the Federation of Blind Muscle Builders of Canada to present you with this plaque.' Jersey Joe, in his excitement, now stood with his back to Dr Parks. 'You have been a constant inspiration . . .'

'*This is it*. The most moving moment of my life,' Dr Parks said. He turned quickly to the compère. 'Can you at least get the bastard to face me?' he whispered.

Gently the compère turned Jersey Joe toward Dr Parks.

'. . . inspiration to us,' he said, wandering off toward the right again. 'It is therefore with great pleasure that I . . . give you this . . . plaque,' he said, offering it to the audience.

'Over here,' Dr Parks said, turning him round again. He blew his nose. 'I'm speechless. Isn't this sensational?' He held the plaque up to the camera. 'When I get home this plaque takes the place of honour among my hundred and fifty-two other plaques and medals given to me by kings, sheiks, pashas, generals, leaders of men, governments, athletic associations and so forth. I—'

Offstage, right, there was a crash.

'OK,' Lake Ontario Jr called out. 'I've got him.'

'And now,' the compère said, 'Bette Dolan!'

Bette told the people how her father had raised her on the teachings of Doc Burt Parks. 'Even before I could walk,' she said, 'he threw me into the pool. Oh, I went under all right,' she added, 'but he shouted at me, swim, baby, swim . . . and you know the rest of *that* story.'

The applause lasted two minutes.

'And now,' Bette said, 'I'd like to do a little something for you.'

Bette Dolan was handed an ordinary hot water bottle and within three minutes she had managed to blow it up and burst it as easily as a balloon.

'She demonstrated wonderful lung power there,' Dr Parks said, 'didn't she?'

'Wow! I'll say.'

'More.'

'Again.'

Afterwards Bette introduced Atuk to Dr Parks. 'Doc Burt,' she said, 'has seven degrees. He's a doctor of philosophy, divinity, naturopathy and goodness knows what else.'

'I'm world-famous,' Dr Parks said, 'all over Canada.'

Yes, Atuk thought, for it seemed to him this was true of many people he had met in Toronto. What was their secret, he wondered.

'I've only been to Eglinton myself,' Atuk said, shaking his hand warmly. 'What college were you at?'

'What's the difference what college? A college is a college. Some college graduates end up digging ditches. It's what you make of yourself that counts in this world, young fellow.'

'That's true,' Atuk said glumly.

'But don't you worry about him, Doc. Atuk's going to be a big success. I've told you that I'm helping him, haven't I?'

'So you have,' Dr Parks said, looking sharply at Atuk.

Atuk blushed.

'He's shooting for the bull's-eye,' Bette said.

'Have to run,' Dr Parks said. 'Off on a Western tour first thing in the morning. But I'm back in the spring, Bette, and I think the sooner you and I have a talk . . .'

'Sure thing. Bye now.'

'You shouldn't have told him you were helping me. He mightn't understand.'

'Doc Burt is so wonderful he understands everything. And you *are* going to be a success now that you've overcome . . . well, you know. I've got such faith in you.' She squeezed his arm. 'Let's go to my place.'

But Atuk spotted Jersey Joe Marchette being interviewed by a television reporter in another corner and he wanted to hear what the strong man had to say. 'In a minute,' he said to Bette, still wondering where he had seen the Negro with the dark glasses before.

Jersey Joe told the reporter that he had been travelling with Doc Burt's troupe on and off for nearly a year now and he was so happy with them that he intended to apply for Canadian citizenship. 'A Negro has a chance in this country,' he said, 'a decent and dignified chance.' He went on to say that he used to be an actor. 'But they type-cast me in New York. I was strictly limited to coloured roles.'

He added that he hoped to play Samson on CBC-TV.

'But Samson was a Hebrew,' the reporter said.

'Now you tell me something,' Jersey Joe said, his tone extremely reasonable, 'if one of them can play Othello in black-face why can't I play Samson?'

'Come on,' Bette said.

I remember, Atuk thought. The man dusting the table at Nancy Gore's. Blind? 'Coming,' he said thoughtfully.

5

Good day. Leafs shut out Beliveau. Twentyman Pulp & Paper up three-quarters of a point. Two swindles, three robberies, and a knifing in the morning paper, but not one Jewy-sounding name among the suspects. Bowels regular and firm.

'It's the Eskimo again.'

But no sooner had Miss Stainsby opened the door than Rory got a strong enough whiff of Atuk to make that remark redundant.

'Can't see him. No time.' Rory dug generously into his pocket. 'Here. But this is the last time. Tell him he must go back to the Bay. Toronto will only break his heart.'

The phone next; his unlisted number.

'Ruby?'

That could only be his father. Panofsky. There were three children. Rory, Goldie, and Leo. You'd think Rory being the only successful one the old man might have a special feeling for him. No. He spent all his love on Leo.

'Thanks for all that food.'

'It's nothing, Pop.'

'So,' Panofsky said snidely, 'and how are things in the Hitler Youth Camp today?'

'The children are fine, if that's what you mean. And there's nothing wrong with employing a German maid.'

Rory had hired Brunhilde and engaged only non-Jewish girls at the office in order to demonstrate that he was utterly free of prejudice. It was not, as one competitor sneered, that he found non-Jewish girls more respectful, more decorative. Wasn't Rory an ardent Zionist? Neither was he, as Michele once said, afraid of Brunhilde. It's true he paid her lavishly and didn't object when her boy friends went into his liquor, but this was only because he wanted her to learn how liberal *some* Jews could be. Michele's distaste for Brunhilde was easy to figure out. Michele couldn't control the kids, Brunhilde could. Oh, my God, the kids! It was Brunhilde's afternoon off and he had promised to take Garth to the park.

It was lovely, it was so soothing, in the park. I must do this more often, Rory thought, as Garth ran off to play and he opened his newspaper at Jean-

Paul McEwen's column. On the opposite page there was a photograph of Bette Dolan emerging from the pool to light the sabbath candles at Rabbi Glenn Seigal's Temple. The much talked about Aquanaut *Oneg Shabat*; he had missed it. Stunning girl, Rory thought. But this reflection was abstract, an aesthetic judgement, not the least bit tinged with guilt or desire. Rory had never been unfaithful to Michele. Even during that dreadfully trying time, following the death of their first-born child, when she had cut him off for six months, he had still not cohabited with another woman. Not that he hadn't had plenty of opportunities. At the time, in fact, he and Harry Snipes, then still a director, were largely responsible for casting the Twentyman Playhouse series. Many actresses, ambitious as they were luscious, arranged to come in for the last appointment of the day. 'I'd do anything to get the part,' more than one said. And Snipes, the boor, would take him aside and say, 'It's nooky time, man. Flip you for who gets the wet deck.'

No: not Rory. He understood Snipes's sort. The eternal Don Juan, so immature that he had to prove himself again and again. Not Rory. He wasn't, for the sake of a fleeting enjoyment, going to leave himself open to blackmail, disease, and possibly a broken home. Before auditioning girls late in the afternoon Rory choked off desire by masturbating. True, even though the series had been finished long since, the habit had somehow stuck with him. But at least he hadn't ended up on the couch. Like Snipes. Rory could handle his own problems.

Funny. Rory hadn't thought about the death of his first-born, Wayne, for a long time. He and Michele, ineffably happy today, had once been touched by tragedy. Fortunately this had only brought them closer together, but at the time . . . Wayne, their first-born, had got off to a bad start. He was underweight. The doctors prescribed vitamins and, as the Peels could well afford it, they administered triple the recommended daily dose. The child put on weight – lots of weight – until, finally, too healthy to live, he died.

Rory, glancing up from his newspaper, saw a cop standing at the edge of the path. His heart began to thump. Suddenly he realized that among all the kids, nurses, and grandmothers at the playground, there was only one grown man. Rory Peel. *Why had he worn his grey suede shoes today?* The cop began to move toward him. Oh, my God. Rory groped for a cigarette, was just about to light it, when he decided, no, it might make him look shifty. He looked up at the towering cop, his grin sickly.

'Hi. Lovely day, isn't it?'

'Sure is.'

The cop began to walk on, but Rory stopped him.

'Thought I'd take an afternoon off from the office.'

'Playing hookey, eh?'

'Ha, ha. Sure am.'

35

In Russia, if his father's tales were to be believed, the cossacks were to be feared. In Canada, a cop was your pal. *Christ; here he comes again.*

'That's my kid over there. Garth. Cute little fella, isn't he?'

'Mm-hm.'

But the cop looked puzzled. He walked to the edge of the path, joined another cop, and began to whisper.

Wait. Rory noticed, for the first time, that he wasn't the only man in the park after all. On a secluded bench under a tree a creamy-faced boy sat with a luscious girl. As Rory turned to look the couple broke apart, flustered. Smoochers. The girl appeared to be somewhat older than the boy . . . and the boy looked awfully familiar. Now where have I seen that face before? Rory must have been staring because, quite suddenly, the boy hid his face in his hands. He had begun to weep quietly.

The cops started down the path.

'Garth, let's go home now.'

'No.'

'Garth, I'm your dad. Now let's go home, darling.'

'Kiss my ass.'

'If you come home now, right now, I'll give you five dollars.'

'Ten.'

'OK.'

Kids are easy, Rory thought, taking Garth by the hand. The trick is to use pyschology.

6

What you dare to dream; dare to do.

The next morning, as usual, Atuk leaped out of bed at seven-thirty and hurried over to his radio. He sat, pencil poised, one eye on the dollar bills stuck to the peg board above, waiting for Derm Gabbard to announce the serial numbers on today's *Lucky Bucks*. If only Atuk could come up with a winning serial number, and make it to the studio before ten a.m., he stood to collect one hundred dollars. This morning, however, he didn't even come close. Never mind. Toronto was so rich in opportunities that an alert Eskimo could even make a start on his fortune while he slept. Atuk kept his radio tuned to CJFD all night, just in case Night Owl phoned to find out if he was listening and offered him a free television set, washing machine or wristwatch with automatic calendar and built-in alarm. As he ate breakfast he memorized the first twenty tunes on the hit parade, not one to be caught off guard should *Guess the Melody* pick his number out of the phone book and offer riches. Because he took the *Standard* each morning he was entitled to a free accident policy and as he had the *Gazette* delivered to his door he was automatically covered against harm by hurricane.

Back on the Bay, Atuk remembered, you could

walk into the wind for miles and you were fortunate indeed if you ran into somebody willing and able to buy you a beer. But in Toronto they stopped just short of paving the streets with gold. Any minute a fortune might drop at your feet. Round one corner The Friendly Loan Company beckoned you to just come in and grab what you wanted, and round another, men with guns drawn unloaded bags of money from an armoured car. A fifty cent purchase at Twentyman's Department Store entitled you to a chit that could get you a free return trip to Rome or the Setting for Ben-Hur, if you won the Lucky Dip. If you signed a five-year lease for an apartment at the Colony then the first six months were free. At the shopping plaza, round the corner from where Atuk lived, the thirty-two-foot yacht on exhibition was being given away by Twentyman Razor Blades for the best jingle submitted by May 1st. Not only that. But each time Atuk joined the rest of the unemployed, and there had never been more in the history of Toronto, to buy bread or a tin of baked beans at the same plaza, he was given a slip to fill out that could win him his own island in the St Lawrence. There *had* to be a winner every week.

So why am I never lucky?

Eskimo luck, he thought, that's my trouble.

This was, beyond a doubt, the blackest time of Atuk's young life. Go back to the Bay, you'll only be corrupted here, said Gore. Rory Peel said, Tell him he must go back to the Bay. Toronto will only break his heart.

Damn damn damn, wasn't he aching for home? A chat with the Old One. His brothers and sisters and cousins. The hunt. But how could he return – a failure? Yesterday the pride and hope of the Elders, today a laughing stock.

—We warned you. An Eskimo should know his place.

—You think they'd give you a chance? A young Eskimo.

No. What you dare to dream; dare to do. He would stay in Toronto and fight it out.

Atuk, freshly resolved, went out for a walk. In Toronto, remember, a fortune could drop at your feet any minute. Today, as always, he carried an Ozo soap wrapper with him on the off chance that he might run into the beautiful, prize-giving Miss Body Odour. Although he had no purchases to make, Atuk zigzagged in and out of the magic eye doors of supermarkets, chain drugstores, and department stores, all the way home, just in case he should be the One Millionth Happy Customer to pass through These Friendly Doors, and therefore be showered with munificence.

Nothing.

Atuk, by this time, was so self-absorbed, such was his misery, that he did not even notice he had wandered into an unfamiliar neighbourhood. He stopped at a strange, very fashionable corner and immediately had to shoulder his way through an enormous crowd. People gaped and wondered aloud as three Twentyman trailer-trucks, escorted by private security police, on motorcycles, sped down the street. Each truck was heavily covered with tarpaulins and bore a shriek of a red sign aloft: STICK OUT YOUR NECK.

I sure do, Atuk thought, and all at once he found himself staring into an art store window. Atuk pressed his nose against the glass to have a closer look at the Eskimo sculpture on display and the price being asked for it. He was spellbound. 'Goddam it,' he said aloud.

Passers-by saw a short Chinese-looking man dancing a jig in the snow and put him down for a drunk.

'I'm rich,' Atuk shouted. 'I'm rich.' And he hurried right over to Rory Peel's office. This time there was no putting him off with a ten-dollar bill.

After Atuk had finished his story, Rory sat for a long while, chin cupped in his hands. 'Give me until tomorrow morning,' he finally said.

Michele was for it; she went for the indigenous cultural angle. Twentyman, amused, said sure.

Atuk was waiting outside the office at eight o'clock in the morning.

'All right,' Rory said. 'I've thought it over. You're on, but—'

Atuk beamed. He did a happy little dance.

'—but only if you let me call the shots. We've got to play this Rory Peel's way.'

'You're the boss,' Atuk said immediately.

I certainly am, Rory thought, feeling a sudden surge of confidence. Superiority. After all, he's only a dumb Eskimo. Almost a coloured man. Rory told Miss Stainsby he was not to be disturbed. He became very masterful, business-like. 'Number one,' he said, 'is there anything in your past we have to worry about?'

Atuk hesitated for only an instant, a suspicious instant, before he smiled and said, 'No.'

'Now look here, if there's anything tell me now. We could be ruined if it came out later.'

I'm safe, Atuk thought. The case was closed long ago. 'There's nothing,' he said. 'I'm clean as a seal's tooth.'

'Seal's tooth. Very good. Colourful. I want you to stick to that sort of idiom in public, Atuk.'

'Shit. You're not talking to a stage Eskimo. Like I don't rub noses any more, you know.'

'I'm talking about one thing only,' Rory said, 'our business image.'

'OK,' Atuk said, 'sure.'

'Good. Next question. What about you and Bette Dolan. Is there anything illicit in your relationship?'

'Bette Dolan,' Atuk said, aghast.

True enough, Rory thought. Everybody knows she's frigid.

'Point number three. There are people we have to watch out for in this town, Atuk. People we don't want for enemies. Say Seymour Bone and Jean-Paul McEwen.'

'It is my creed,' Atuk said, his face shining, 'that we must love one another or die.'

'Very good. Nicely put. Now about Bone. He sets the cultural tone in this town. Flatter him. Jean-Paul McEwen will be more difficult.' Rory broke off. He turned on both water taps in the bathroom, disconnected the phone, lowered the window and turned on the radio. 'She's our moral watch-dog sort of. She looks out for lapses in our ethical conduct. Her spies and operatives are everywhere. Disguised too. Take Twentyman, for instance. One day coming out of his club he was stopped by an old cripple with flies on his face. "Dime for a cup of coffee, mister?" Naturally Twentyman brushed the vermin-ridden fool aside. Next morning, opening the paper at McEwen's column, he reads, "Hard-Hearted Buck Twentyman . . ." That bitch's spies are everywhere, Atuk, everywhere. We must be on our guard.'

The next afternoon Atuk signed over twenty-five per cent of Esky Enterprises to Rory. Together they planned the poetry reading at the Cha-Cha-Chow-Mein. The first name to be put on the guest list was that of Professor Norman Gore.

'Without his help,' Atuk said, 'I would be nothing.'

Part 2   Eskimo Tycoon

1

In the unheated cellar of the Cha-Cha-Chow-Mein Restaurant, where *group sixty-one* met on Thursday nights, no liquor, indeed only Nescafé, was available, but the thoughtful management had set down an empty vodka bottle on each checkered tablecloth that was at least suggestive of hip depravity. A long angular black-haired girl in a loose green sweater and a shiny black skirt climbed on to the high stool to sing *Manitob-hi-yay* and Goldie buttered a bagel and resumed her knitting.

Goldie Panofsky, plump and rosy-cheeked, wore shimmering golden slacks and a striped lemon blouse buttoned tightly over a generous spill of bosom. Her brown hair was done up in the Bardot-style and her long nails were painted steel-grey. Goldie glared contemptuously at Bette Dolan, seated ringside in a white satin sheath. Then she waved and called yoo-hoo when she spied her father struggling through the darkness, his sociology text

43

books still in hand. 'Like you're late, Paw,' she said.

'He's started already?'

'No. But he hasn't stopped staring at me all night.'

Panofsky chuckled. '*Ca, alors,*' he said.

'Honest, Paw. Like I should drop down dead.'

So Panofsky risked a glance at him – Atuk – and it appeared to be true. The fat brown-skinned hunter with the slit eyes smiled and dipped his head.

'He recognizes me,' Panofsky said, 'from when Professor Gore introduced us.'

'He's staring at me. *Dig?*'

'*Narishkeit.*'

Rory approached Atuk, whispered diffidently in his olive ear, and the two men went behind the platform to wait for the long angular singer to step down. Atuk winked at Goldie. Shyly, but unmistakably.

'Well, Mr Doubting Thomas?'

'A twitch. He's nervous. Just look around you, my God!'

There was, it was true, a sense of occasion in the cellar. Atuk, after all, had disappeared from sight for more than a month, and during that time Rory had been busy. Very busy.

Norman Gore waved at Atuk. 'He looks tired, Nancy,' the professor said. The current rumour, one among many, was that the Eskimo poet had sent to the Bay for his family and that as many as eighteen

44

brothers, sisters, aunts and cousins were now staying with him. 'If that's the case,' Gore told the party at his table, 'then his kindness is misplaced. He's an artist. The burden could crush him.'

Debutantes, young sports car enthusiasts of Forest Hill, students, booking agents for rival coffee bars and delicatessens aside, many of Toronto's cultural tastemakers sat silent and severe in the darkness. Bushy head of red hair dishevelled, chin sunken to his chest, massive Seymour Bone turned to his wife with a smile. 'I'm appalled,' he said, with a sweep of his small melting hand, 'histrionically speaking, even on the level of . . .'

'Darling,' his wife said, 'your tie,' and while he feigned disinterest she wiped his chin with her handkerchief.

Harry Snipes scrawled notes hurriedly with a pen that had a built-in flashlight. He was, they said, writing a profile on Atuk for *Metro*. Only two tables away sat a glowering Jean-Paul McEwen and many, the bored and the merely malicious, were hoping for an altercation. McEwen, the most widely-read columnist in Toronto, was anathema to Buck Twentyman of course and, like Bone, a nationally known television personality.

'In my opinion,' Jean-Paul McEwen said, offering Bone a Schimmelpenninck, 'he's a fraud, but just for the hell of it, just to show you how this town can be taken, I'm going to blow the bastard up before . . .'

Seymour Bone began to breathe quickly and under the table his wife passed him a banana. 'It's already peeled,' she said.

As Atuk stepped on to the platform everybody began to chatter. Most of them, it's safe to say, were familiar with Atuk's best-loved poem, the one that had appeared in his book, the national advertisements, and that he had read in the same cellar shortly after he had first come to Toronto.

> *I go hunt bear in white dawn,*
> *good spirit come with me.*
> *I go fish in silver twilight,*
> *good spirit come with me.*
> *Over the white crust soon comes*
> *forever night*
> *good spirit,*
> *O, spirit,*
> *stay with me.*

Press photographers bore down on the small squat hunter.

'This night will go down in literary history. Like the time Leacock . . .'

Panofsky squinted, trying to roll a cigarette in the dim light. 'You think I ought to go up to say hello to Bone?'

'Endsville,' Goldie said. 'I don't want you to invite him. I—'

'*Quiet, Everybody!*'

46

His gesture modest but firm, Atuk indicated that there would be no more pictures.

Atuk.

Gore warned the party at his table not to expect too much from the reading. Continued exposure to Toronto had not done the Eskimo any good. The poet had, he said, fallen in with Harry Snipes, the most notorious of Canada's middle-aged angries, and, as a result, his latest work, though not without an impact of its own, had lost a certain arctic simplicity.

Atuk retreated a little from under the spotlight, smiled shyly, coughed, and began to read.

> *Twentyman Fur Company,*
> *I have seen the best seal hunters of my*
> *generation putrefy raving die from tuberculosis,*
> *Massey, you square,*
> *eskimos don't rub noses any more and the cats*
> *around Baffin Bay dig split-level houses.*
> *Listen to me, Pearson,*
> *a house is not a home,*
> *an igloo is not a pad.*
> *And you, Diefenbaker, can kiss my ass*
> *where holy most holy pea-soup hockey players have*
> *rumbled.*
> *Canada, wake up, you're all immigrants to me:*
> *my people are living like niggers.*

'You disgusting son-of-a-bitch,' Rory said, 'from now on you clear every poem with me.'

'But listen, listen to them, will you.'

The applause was deafening.

'That's not the point,' Rory said. 'You took Twentyman's name in vain.'

Still protesting, Rory was thrust back as admirers gathered round to congratulate Atuk.

'Is much good you all like,' Atuk said. 'My heart fills.'

Panofsky had been doubtful, even as he shouldered through to Atuk, that the Eskimo would accept his invitation over all the others that were being offered. But Atuk was delighted.

'It's not much of a *soirée*,' Panofsky said. 'Some snacks. A little wine.'

Atuk stepped close enough to Goldie to sniff her. 'Did you enjoy yourself?' he asked.

'Ai. A ball.'

Atuk smiled blissfully as Rory pushed through to him again. 'Hey,' Rory said, 'you can't go to my father's house. You're supposed to be coming to the party at my place.'

Atuk pulled Rory aside. 'Of course I'm coming to your house. But you don't want me to be the first to arrive. A man of my stature ought to make an entrance.'

'Sure,' Rory said, suspicious, 'but—'

'You take Bette with you,' Atuk said, nudging him in the ribs. 'I'll be along as soon as possible.'

'OK. If you like,' Rory said, obviously pleased.

Bette was struggling into her coat.

'Here,' Rory said, 'let me help you.'

'Maybe,' Bette said, 'we can help each other.'

Rory, flustered, said, 'My name's Peel.' He took her arm. 'I'm Jewish,' he added hastily.

2

How they all managed to squeeze into his place, who most of them were, was a puzzle to Panofsky. Fortunately, many had brought bottles. Panofsky and Snipes sat together at the kitchen table, a bottle of brandy between them.

'I know very well,' Snipes said, 'that a lot of slobs in this country have put down Twentyman for a reactionary lug and a louse – I like knocking him myself – but I've seen the man up close. Twentyman is first and foremost a Canadian.'

A photographer moved from one room to another, asking questions and taking pictures. 'Anybody here seen Mr Atuk?'

'Sorry, no.'

Snipes set up a stall in the hall and began to peddle books of his poetry. He cornered Norman Gore.

'You dry academics,' Snipes said, 'give me one long pain fart-wise, the way you analyse a poem line by line, image by image. Like a disease.'

Gore was delighted. 'Go ahead, please. The creative mind—'

'Look here, Gore, even TV commercials scan. I

have a better way to recognize a poet. I look to see if he has that look of doom in his eyes.'

Somebody in the room above began thumping on the ceiling.

'My son Leo,' Panofsky said with a gentle smile. 'He's hungry, I suppose.'

'Sure,' Snipes said, turning to the others, 'wring your hands, scratch your noggins, but the trouble with us lard-bottomed, spoon-fed Canadians is we live in a mealy-mouthed atmosphere of mumble-mumble in national purpose. When do we ever get angry?'

'Excuse me,' the photographer said. 'Have you seen Mr Atuk anywhere?'

'Why don't you ask our hostess, Miss Panofsky?'

'Can't seem to find her anywhere either.'

'The trouble with Canadians,' Snipes continued, 'is we're too damn conventional. I'll bet if I were to do something spontaneous like, just for the sake of argument, if I were to expose myself right now you'd all be shocked.'

'Margie,' Nancy Gore called. 'Come here. Quickly.'

Norman Gore rose. 'Good God,' he said, 'it's four a.m.'

Once Panofsky had said goodbye to everyone, after they had all gone, he realized that Atuk and his daughter were nowhere to be seen. He found them in the bedroom. Atuk lay with his head on Goldie's lap. She was stroking his straight black hair. 'Quiet,' she said. 'He's in Dreamsville.'

But Atuk, his hunter's ear keen as ever, jumped up.

'I apologize,' Atuk said. 'We've been talking, no more. I assure you nothing out of the ordinary has happened.'

'And I assure you,' Panofsky said, 'that I'm no prude.' Smiling thinly, he added: '*Au plaisir*, Atuk.'

The toilet door was open, but the place was occupied. '*Mon Dieu.*' Harry Snipes lay on the floor, a rubber band twisted around his arm and a needle on his lap. Panofsky held his hand to his cheek.

'It's nothing,' Atuk said, hastily gathering Snipes into his arms.

'Watch out you don't hurt yourself,' Goldie said. 'If you know what I mean.'

She went to the window to watch Atuk dump Snipes into the black Thunderbird and drive off.

'Goldie, he's not for you. I—'

The thumping from above started again.

'You stop that banging this minute,' Goldie shouted, 'or it's back to the flip-factory with you.' She began to gather all the food scraps into a pail. 'I guess Leo must be starving,' she said.

'Atuk's not for you. I wouldn't stand for it. Think of what Rory would say.'

'Conning tower to pilot,' Goldie said, 'conning tower to pilot.'

It was a game Panofsky loathed, but all the same he said, 'Come in, conning tower.'

'Join me on Cloud-9. Like I'm swinging, man.'
'*Mazel tov.*'

Panofsky and Leo were out all night again. In fact, Goldie had finished her breakfast by the time they returned the next morning. She could tell they had been doing research for her father's thesis because both of them were wearing their surgical coats.

'Man,' Goldie said, 'I wish you and Leo would kick the habit. Like you're riding your luck too hard. One night the fuzz will get you.'

Panofsky grunted. He gave Leo a kick. 'Upstairs with you,' he said.

'What did he do, Paw?'

'Never mind. But next time,' Panofsky said, climbing on to a chair to shake a fist under his son's nose, 'next time, Mr Butter-Fingers . . .'

Leo began to sob brokenly.

'Paw,' Goldie said.

'All right,' Panofsky's tone became conciliatory, paternal. 'There's a big *goy* funeral this afternoon. Catholic. If you're good you can come.'

'Catholic's my favourite,' Leo said, wiping his tears.

'Now upstairs I said.' Turning to Goldie, he seemed to notice for the first time that she was dressed to go out. 'And where would you be off to?' he asked.

'I'm not seeing him again, Paw. All right? Good enough?'

'All I want to warn you is that if Rory—'

'What if I told you he and Rory were very close. Partners, in fact.'

'Business is one thing, personal life another. Now where are you going?'

'To have lunch with a girl friend.'

3

When Atuk had been a rough but impressionable Baffin Bay boy the Old One – described in a prize-winning National Film Board short as 'wise and leathery, his neck laced by many winds, the face bitten by decades of frost, and his eyes accustomed to the hungers of the long night'—had taken him on his lap and told him, 'For an Eskimo boy to make his mark in this world, Atuk, he must be brighter, better, and faster than other boys.' Far from forgetting, Atuk had modelled his life on this precept. So that morning he rose as usual at 6.30 a.m., ate a three-day-old crust of bread dipped in whale oil, washed it down with an ice-cold Pepsi and, even though thoughts of Goldie made for a delightful ache in his groin, set right down to work.

A tour of the basement factory, before the others had risen, satisfied him that production was slowing down again. His relàtives, indolent to the bone, were in constant need of a whip-hand over them, otherwise they abandoned their work benches each morning to snooze. The demands for sculpture from London, Paris, New York, and even Tokyo, far exceeded his family's basement production, but bringing down more relatives from Baffin Bay was no answer. Only the laziest were left. Another consideration was that the indoctrination period was too wearying. 'Atuk, I am frightened. It is winter. Yet every twelve hours there is the miracle of light. Are the Gods angry?' Neither would he put up once more with ignorant nieces breaking up cigars to spice the stew or with gluttonous, ever-thirsty uncles boiling his tooled leather belts in the soup and pouring anti-freeze into the punch bowl. No. There was another answer. Moulds. Machinery. Mass production. He would have to look around for a plant. The family could be moved by night as usual and nobody need know what was being produced inside. Rory could be counted on to work out the camouflage and other details.

The newspapers arrived.

UNEMPLOYMENT FIGURES LEAP UPWARDS, Atuk read in the *Gazette*, but turning the page he felt gratified to see that the Liberal Party, aroused, promised a Canadian flag once they returned to office. At the bottom of the page he read that there was a further development in the DEW LINE DISAPPEARANCE case. The story, off the front pages for months, had to do with an American army intelligence colonel who had disappeared while on a tour of inspection of the Arctic defence lines. A kidnapping by Russian agents was suspected. But after seven weeks of investigation the RCMP had failed to come up with a single clue and now, it appeared, the FBI had been called in on, the *Gazette* pointed out, a co-operative basis. Not so, Atuk read in a front-page article by Harry Snipes. 'Indeed, what we are seeing is yet another instance of Uncle Sam the Brinkman riding roughshod over our own national interests.' In the *Gazette*, Atuk saw that Rabbi Glenn Seigal had announced that he had been able to secure Jerry Lewis to give readings from the Book of Esther at the up-and-coming Israeli Bond drive. Atuk snorted and turned to the financial pages. His investments, considering the present state of affairs in Canada, were not doing too badly. He also found the coverage of his reading for *group sixty-one* entirely satisfactory. Jean-Paul McEwen, in her column in the *Standard*, was especially complimentary – or was she writing tongue-in-cheek? Is she poking fun at me? Atuk paused, he pondered. No, he thought, I'm just being touchy. A thin-skinned Eskimo. He made a note for Miss Stainsby to send McEwen a bottle of perfume. Perfume? McEwen? No; better a case of Scotch.

Upstairs, the Old One began to stir. Atuk sniffed nervously. He had no desire to cross with him this morning.

There was, of course, plenty of mail.

Bruno of Ottawa wished to photograph him. Good, Atuk thought, and he jotted down a note on top of the letter for Miss Stainsby. Harry Snipes wanted to see him about a possible television series. Atuk was interested, he went for the idea, but he marked the letter 'request more details', for he was not going to get involved in another of those co-production deals, pilot films, percentages, work now and maybe, get paid later. Elsewhere, the president of Educational Folk Toys, Inc., was enthusiastic about the Esky-Doll but he wanted to get together to discuss royalties, possible promos, and the Eskybilly disc tie-up, before he went into production. Well, Rory could handle that one too. A lady in Regina had sent Atuk a pair of knitted socks. They looked dreadful. Flashy. Negroid, he thought. Atuk held them over the wastepaper basket and then had second thoughts. Treated properly this was just the kind of heart-warming story that would make a big splash in the western papers. 'Develop,' Atuk wrote on top of the lady's letter, 'Hickville-wise.'

Somebody was coming down the steps. Atuk sniffed tentatively. Yes, damn it, it's the Old One. I can't face his reproaches this morning, he thought. If he feels so badly why in the hell doesn't he return to the Bay? Atuk grabbed a pencil, some paper, and slipped into the toilet. 'Atuk to Stainsby,' he wrote, 'poem, esk. style, broad. rights, CBC Anthology, pay, min. $100. Pub. rights, McAllister's Fort., min. pay, ditto.'

O plump and delicious one
here in land of so short night
me
alone,
humble,
hungering

A pounding on the door.

'Who in the hell is it?'

'Me. Ti-Lucy. Let me in. *Quick*, brother.'

'Goddam it, I'm working.'

'But if we use the sink you are angry with us.'

'All right. OK.' Atuk held the door open for her. 'You people. Christ!'

'Will we be allowed the great magic tonight, brother?'

'You heard what I told the boys last night. Only if there's an upswing in production. Only if. You tell them that. And would you mind shutting the door after you, please.'

Rory, as he anticipated, phoned at ten sharp.

'Well you certainly fouled things up last night,' Rory said, 'didn't you?'

'How come? Did you read McEwen this morning? She thinks I'm great.'

'Don't be so sure. Why didn't you come to my place?'

'I was ill. Too much excitement. Too much drink.'

'Bone and McEwen sat here waiting around until three in the morning. I nearly went out of my mind.

Do you want to start out by making enemies of two of the most influential figures in the country?'

'Certainly not.'

'Haven't you heard of the telephone?'

'I passed out. Honestly, Rory.'

'Just thank your lucky stars for Bette. She appeased them. She charmed them. She told them that she's been helping you for quite a while now.'

'Did she say how?'

'No. Listen here, Atuk, you put me on the spot like last night once more and—'

'Never again, Rory. I swear. And don't worry about Bone. I'll send him a note.'

Bette phoned next.

'I passed out,' Atuk said. 'I'm sorry.'

'Are you coming to my place tonight?'

'Sure.'

Atuk worked until noon and then got into his coat.

'I had thought,' the Old One said, blocking his path, 'that you were going to break bread with me today.'

'Sorry. I've got an important engagement.' Atuk took down the bar, he unbolted the door, and opened the locks one by one. 'Now don't look at me like that. This is strictly business.'

4

Bone. Seymour Bone.

If Bette Dolan swam into the heart of a nation with one mighty effort then Seymour Bone, another national figure, had to plan, connive, claw, insult, lust and rage for years before he was recognized. Dominion-wide.

Out of the west he came on flat broad feet in 1945, the rebellious, ambitious, acme-ridden son of a successful Presbyterian salesman. Out of the west to conquer Toronto; the cruel capital. A fat ungainly redheaded boy, Bone had abandoned his native plain because his ideas, his style of life, were considered too wildly bohemian by the people there. Bone openly read Samuel Butler, he advocated drinking on Sundays, quoted George Bernard Shaw, and subscribed to journals such as *John O'London's*. In a Rotary-sponsored debate, actually to do with the United Nations, he came out flatly for premarital relations. But at the University of Toronto, Bone, to his dismay, discovered that his ideas were not considered very, very shocking. He fitted in nowhere. The intellectuals put him down for a backward, if amusing bumpkin, and the others found him a bore. Lonely, broken-hearted, he began to eat prodigiously, mostly bananas, and felt himself an utter failure until he was taken in hand by Ruthy

Rosenthal. Ruthy, outspoken daughter of a Toronto pants manufacturer, was even more rebellious than Bone.

At the age of twelve, already an unbeliever, she said to her grandfather, 'And whom, may I ask, did Cain marry?'

'Communist bitch.'

Persecuted for her ideas, Ruthy was driven to further extremes of rebellion. She began to eat bacon. She refused to attend her grandmother's funeral. 'As I am already an atheist,' she said, 'it would be hypocrisy for me.'

'But she's your *bubba*, when you were a little *cacker* who wiped you?'

'I won't be swayed by false sentiment.'

Ruthy thought it was endearing of Seymour Bone, on first meeting, to think he could shock her by lending her his copy of *Jurgen*. It was in a plain brown wrapper.

'*Jurgen*, Cabell. Sweetie-pie,' she said, 'haven't you even heard of Henry Miller yet?'

Bone took *The Tropic of Cancer* back to his room, his eyes almost popping out of his head as he read. There are, he had to admit, gaps in my knowledge. Ruthy filled the hole with Freud, *Fanny Hill*, *Partisan Review*, Trotsky, Auden, and others. They became an inseparable campus couple and, the day after graduation, were married. A civil ceremony of course.

Bone married Ruthy because:

(1) This, he hoped, would prove his ultimate liberation from a provincial anti-Semitic family.

(2) Let's face it, the girl, being a Jewess, would be forever in his debt. She could never be unfaithful. On the contrary. She would be respectful, grateful.

(3) He had come to adore Jewish cooking even more than bananas.

Ruthy married Bone because:

(1) She wished to give her family a final slap in the face.

(2) It would prove – especially to sceptical friends who predicted she would end up married to a dentist with a house in the suburbs – that she wasn't ghetto-bound.

(3) Being a *goy*, he couldn't be as smart as she was. She could direct and control him.

Bone, who had expected to feast nightly on herrings, knishes, cholent, pastramis and briskets, was served hard-boiled eggs or, on special occasions, sea food.

'I'm not a chauvinist,' Ruthy said.

Sea food made her vomit but she was battling to overcome this, like other narrowing prejudices she had inherited.

'I admire your spirit,' Bone said.

Ruthy, who had looked forward to sharing her bed with a bullish *goy*, a brute, a destroyer, a rape artist, instead of an inhibited good-Jewish-boy, found that Seymour was a once-a-week rabbit.

Each time this unconventional marriage was

about to break up it was saved by the couple's conventional families. Ruthy's father would say, 'A mixed marriage can never work,' and thereby drive her back into Seymour's arms. Seymour's mother would say, 'If you leave her we will forgive all and take you back,' and send him lumbering back into her arms.

And meanwhile Seymour struggled. Because he liked going to plays and sleeping in late, he decided to become a drama critic, but nobody would hire him. So Seymour Bone, investing the last of his inheritance, decided to put out a critical journal of his own written entirely by himself and Ruthy: *The Genius*. It did not do well the first year, even as a give-away to actors, writers, and producers. But the second year a miracle happened. Within one week, both *Time* and the London *Spectator* decided to do humorous columns about culture in Canada and chose Bone's journal as a logical take-off point. Very few people in Canada realized that their struggling, no-saying critic was being ridiculed. On the contrary. Most people were impressed.

'It doesn't matter what we think,' a realistic CBC producer said. 'If the London *Spectator* feels he's worth writing about, we ought to give him an opportunity.'

'How come *Time* never quotes our drama critic?' a newspaper publisher asked.

So Seymour Bone, critic, was born. He overate so much before attending his first play for the

Standard that, though he was enjoying himself immensely, he simply had to flee before the end of the first act.

BONE STOMPS OUT, one newspaper headline boomed over a four-column photograph of the critic seated in the second row, his face a map of suffering and distaste. CANADA'S RUDEST DRAMA CRITIC, another headline ran. The story was picked up by Canadian Press and ran across the country. Bone went to the theatre constipated and woke up a national figure. But his newly-won reputation was also to ruin his pleasure for years to come. For the truth was that Bone was delighted by most plays, specially if they were full of salty jokes or good-looking girls, but he felt that if he didn't walk out on every second one people would say he was going soft. So walk out he did, often returning in disguise the next night to surreptitiously enjoy the rest of the play.

Bone, now a national figure, was immediately offered a CBC television panel show, *Crossed Swords*. He blossomed forth as a sort of reverse Liberace. The Rudest, Most Outspoken Entertainer in Canada. He talked about his column on television and wrote about his show in his column. His column was widely read. But as Bone's celebrity increased, even as his insults grew more shrill, he became personally unpopular. Nobody asked him to parties any more. In fact, the first party he had been asked to in nine months was the one Rory Peel gave in honour of

Atuk. When the little Eskimo freak didn't turn up Bone was livid; he swore vengeance. All the next morning he was in a black mood, so that when Ruthy entered his study at noon, bringing him lunch, she expected another angry outburst. But Seymour was on the phone.

'Operator. Get me Montreal, please. Rod Murchison at the *Sun*.' Seymour peeled a banana while he waited. 'Hello, Rod. Bone here. I merely wish to relate how prodigiously I enjoyed your column this week. It had a telling corporeity to it. Most rare.'

'Gee thanks, Seymour.'

'Not in the least. Oh, I have a little item for your next column. You might say Seymour Bone, Canada's leading critic, will be coming to Montreal for the week-end to peruse French theatre. Oh, and you could add this time he doesn't want anybody to know he'll be staying at the Laurentian Hotel. He will read no manuscripts by would-be playwrights.'

'Gee, Seymour, did lots of guys bother you last time you were here?'

'No,' Bone said, stiffening, 'but you can never tell, can you? Oh, one more thing. You could add that in Seymour Bone's opinion,' he said, finding the sentence he had just underlined in his airmail edition of the *New Statesman*, 'the kitchen sink is sunk.'

'Ha, ha, very good, Seymour.'

'Thank you. See you, anon. Bye now.'

Ruthy set Seymour's tray down on the desk.

'You'll be late for the studio if you don't hurry,' she said.

Seymour began to eat hastily.

'Atuk, the Eskimo, is going to be on the show this week.' Seymour grinned. 'He's hardly our intellectual equal, I'm afraid, but he does have a following.'

Ruthy, aware of the malice implicit in Seymour's grin, pitied the Eskimo already. Seymour would pulverize him.

5

Panofsky lifted a pail off the stove and carried the still steaming stew upstairs to Leo.

'As soon as you're finished put on the white jacket.'

Leo looked up, his eyes glazed. 'Uh?'

'We're going out,' Panofsky said. 'More work. Research.'

Panofsky went to the window to see if Goldie was still pacing up and down outside. He was just in time to see the black Thunderbird pull up. Atuk opened the door for Goldie, and the two of them sped off.

If Ruby only knew what I go through here, Panofsky thought. Aw, he's probably still in bed.

But Rory Peel was in the kitchen, on the phone to his office. 'Miss Stainsby,' he said, 'you can assure

Twentyman that before our campaign is done everybody, but everybody, in this country will be asking
themselves what does STICK OUT YOUR NECK
mean.' What I'm worried about, he thought, is
what happens when they find out. 'Should be at the
office in forty-two minutes.'

Rory hurried round to the back of the house to
see how the workmen were getting on and was horrified to see Springhorn watching from his side of the
hedge. 'Oh, hi, Springhorn,' he said nervously.

' 'Morning, Peel.' Springhorn indicated the workmen with an ambiguous smile. 'Busy, busy, eh,
Peel?'

'They're laying the foundation for a swimming
pool. So help me God they are.'

'Uh-huh.'

'Can I give you a lift into town, perhaps?'

'Naw. I'll just stand here and watch. Foundation
runs kinda deep, doesn't it, Peel?'

'Sorry. I'm in a dreadful hurry.'

What could go wrong now, Rory thought, driving
into town. Nothing. He was protected against all
mishaps and the new Twentyman deal was his
biggest yet. Personal embarrassments? Goldie, back
at college, was out of harm's way and his father had
promised to cut out the crazy stuff. His research.

Nurse Tomkins, maternity ward, Protestant Temperance, started. 'Oh, it's you, Dr Zale.'

'Yes,' Panofsky said, 'it's only me.'

Leo grunted.

'And how's the little Edwards child today?' Panofsky asked.

Nurse Tomkins handed Panofsky the chart.

'Capital,' Panofsky said. 'Capital. Dr Shub . . . ?' He passed the chart to Leo.

Outside, Atuk geared down to second.

'What is it?' Goldie asked.

But Atuk was staring at the billboard. Another one, the largest he had seen.

STICK OUT YOUR NECK

'Next time I see Buck,' Atuk said, 'I'll ask him what it's all about.'

Buck Twentyman rose with a smile.

'Glad to have you with us,' Twentyman said.

He had chosen Derm 'Gabby' Gabbard over all the other television pitchmen in Canada for the prized job of compère of STICK OUT YOUR NECK because of his incomparably wholesome manner: Canada trusted him.

'Glad to *be* with you, sir,' Derm said, smiling.

Blindfolded, Derm was led to a black limousine by Twentyman and driven off to a studio in the woods. The security guards saluted Twentyman, doublechecked Derm's pass, unlocked the gates, the outer and inner studio doors, and finally the vault. Derm's blindfold was removed at last.

Twentyman pulled the curtain. 'There it is,' he said. 'Your equipment.'

'Golly!' Derm passed his hand lovingly over the ice-blue steel. 'It's ring-a-ding,' he said.

'The bushel with a million bucks will be on the table over here . . . with the guards . . . and over here, the equipment with the contestant. Well?'

'If this show doesn't bring you the highest ratings in the country I'll eat my chapeau,' Derm said.

'But you don't look entirely convinced,' Twentyman said.

'Well, sir, to be frank, ah . . . well, there is *one* area of doubt in my mind. Where will you get a contestant?'

'You just let me worry about that,' Twentyman said.

Atuk was late getting to the office.

'Any messages?' he asked Miss Stainsby.

'Bette Dolan phoned. Three times.'

'Anything else?' Atuk asked.

'Norman Gore called. He wants to know if you've given up night school altogether.'

'Ha, ha, ha.'

Professor Gore stopped Panofsky in the hall.

'Have you seen the evening papers?' he asked. 'Isn't it disgraceful?'

'You mean Snipes asking for an import quota on American magazines?'

'No. Certainly not. I mean our subservient, so-called government playing footsie with the FBI in the Arctic.'

'Don't you think we ought to co-operate with the Americans?' Panofsky asked, bored.

'Co-operation is one thing and domination is another. The trouble with those boys is they see commies under every bed. Surely, *you* don't go for that cock-and-bull story about their colonel having been kidnapped by Russian agents?'

'He did disappear, didn't he?'

'The man had no right investigating *our* defences in the first place. Probably he got drunk one night and fell down an ice crevice.'

'Probably? He certainly did. So why worry?'

'Why? Haven't you any national pride? They step all over us.' Professor Gore suddenly smiled. 'There I go losing my temper again. Oh, say, you will be coming on Friday, won't you?'

'I'm looking forward to it immensely, sir.'

Just about anybody who was anybody was going to Professor Gore's on Friday night. Even Atuk would be there.

The Old One took down the bar, unbolted the door, and opened the locks one by one.

'Enter in peace,' the Old One said.

'Hi,' Atuk said. 'How's everything?'

'They are all gathered around the box and waiting. There is much tension among them for you failed them yesterday. The Old One strongly recommends the magic for tonight.'

'I told them only if they work hard. I—'

'Of work they have done their fill. For this I give my word.'

Atuk went into the living-room and saw for himself how they all sat huddled and expectant round the box. 'Have you been good?' he asked.

'We have been good.'

Only Ignak failed to reply.

'Have you worked hard and long while Atuk, who cares not a reindeer's knuckle for his own safety, has rushed hither and thither among the many white, washed, and unfriendly ones, always in your interest?'

'Yes,' they chanted. 'Yes.'

Ti-Lucy, her eyes shining, brought Atuk the production figures. She removed his shoes and put on his slippers. Atuk grunted. Ti-Lucy poured him a snifter of brandy and lit his cigar.

'Tonight, then,' Atuk said, 'I shall plead for the magic. Bring me the sheet with the craziness upon it.'

Ti-Lucy brought Atuk the *Gazette* and opened it at the page he wanted. 'Turn off the lights,' he said.

'Silence,' Ti-Lucy said.

'Sh.'

Atuk went into his trance. Stumbling, swaying, eyes rolling, he wandered round the room. The others watched hopefully, afraid, tears rolling down their cheeks. Except, Atuk noticed, for Ignak.

'Oh . . . oh . . . I'm beginning to feel the power.' Ti-Lucy cried out. Moose groaned.

'Ai,' Atuk called. 'Aiii-aii.' He backed up against the window and felt behind the curtain with his hands. 'Aii.' With a sudden sweep of his arm, he said, 'Oh, Mighty One, let there be sound for my flock.'

There was sound and Atuk saw that it was good. He counted to five and called out, 'Let there be pictures, Mighty One, for my hard workers. Let the wavy lines form moving pictures. Bring us—'

Atuk broke off, breathing heavily. He waited a little.

'. . . bring us a Dupont Special with Frank Sinatra . . .'

'Oh!'

'. . . Dinah Shore . . .'

'Zowie!'

'. . . Elvis Presley, the Negro with one eye, and Joey Bishop . . .'

'Ay!'

'. . . bring us songs, dances, fill us with laughter.'

'It is too much, Atuk. We burst.'

'Give us this day many girls with long, delicious legs and leaping breasts uncovered.'

The boys began to stamp their feet. Moose stood on his head.

'Look, it is here!'

'Long live Atuk! Maker of miracles!'

'Amen!'

'It is nothing, nothing, my sweet children.' Atuk reached for his snifter of brandy. He took a sip. 'Why, let the Sinatra be followed by disaster pictures of foreign lands . . .'

'Yowie!'

'. . . singing soap-boxes . . . tobacco-sticks that taste like tobacco-sticks should . . . dancing beer bottles . . . empty girdles . . .'

Mush-Mush rolled over on the floor and kicked his legs.

'. . . and will you work even harder tomorrow, children?'

'Yes! Yes! Yes!'

'. . . and the Jack Paar Show, then, to be followed by . . . the late, late movie . . .'

'And the lady with the funny fur hat on the horse. Please, Atuk.'

'Yes, and that too, for Atuk will not be with you until the sun sets twice. For he must make long and dangerous journey over the week-end.'

'I will pack the little white balloons for him,' Ti-Lucy said.

'They are *not* balloons,' Atuk said. 'Who's been blowing those things up again?'

Mush-Mush hid behind a chair. Ignak rose to leave the room.

'What's ailing you?' Atuk asked.

'I'm tired, *miracle-maker*. Good night.'

'Don't look for trouble, kid.'

'I'm not. I'm too bright for that.'

'Stay that way.'

'Conning tower to pilot, conning tower to pilot.'

'All right. Come in, conning tower.'

'Like I'm going to the movies with Freda tomorrow. I think maybe I'll stay the night with her.'

Mush-Mush stared at his favourite commercial, the one that showed the amazing transformation in the white man after he had taken the little white pill. How his head opened to reveal pounding hammers and his transparent stomach filled with quick action relief arrows. 'Oh,' he said. 'Oh.'

Atuk poured himself another brandy. When the third news item came on he started. Suddenly, he was very alert. The hunter. Three FBI agents hurried up the steps to a building in Ottawa. Not far behind came Sgt Jock Wilson.

6

Sgt Jock Wilson felt bad about what he had done, for he had been inordinately fond of Atuk, and yet, and yet, how he had yearned for the fleshpots of Toronto.

The truth was Jock was still a young fellow and he had had his fill of handing out rough justice in fifty below zero weather. What he had dreamt of out on the Bay, what he had lusted for during the endless night, was the warmth and type of work available in Toronto. So he was delighted, actually tingling with excitement, when Col Smith-Williams summoned him to his office for, Jock dared to hope, his reward.

'Jocko, you're not going back to the Bay. We need you here. Anti-subversive work.'

'Good show,' Jock said at once.

But when the Colonel went on to outline the nature of Jock's new assignment the young man's shoulders slumped, his cheeks reddened, he began to stammer. 'Damn it all,' he said at last, 'not really up my street, is it, sir?'

Jock reminded the Colonel of his many manly achievements. He alluded to his marksmanship medal and his ability as a horseman. But Col Smith-Williams was not impressed. He cut Jock short.

'I'm going to give it to you straight from the shoulder,' the Colonel said. 'Things aren't what they used to be.' He went on to explain how all the services must now adjust to the challenge of the nuclear age. When he, Col Smith-Williams, had first served his country, actually as a Captain in the Black Watch during World War I, the military life had been straightforward. At Vimy, by George, you got your orders to go over the top, shot the first enlisted man through the head, and over the top everybody else went. Today things were different.

Mighty different. The RCAF was almost entirely without aeroplanes and men who had once ruled the skies of Malta were now working as night watchmen at American-run missile bases. The only active duty the army had seen in donkey's years was when two divisions were hired out to one Hymie Slotnick to make a Western in Alberta. How many citizens knew that the Royal Canadian Navy's fighting ships were only taken out of mothballs once in the last five years, and that was for a *Vogue* magazine feature on Canadian fashions that was never even published. The RCMP, if it was to survive, would have to adjust too.

'The FBI,' Colonel Smith-Williams said, 'has just outfoxed us in our own back yard. I don't mind telling you, Jocko, the Dew line thing sticks like a bone in my throat. I want some action. I want it right here in Toronto. Go to it, man.'

And that's how come Sgt Jock Wilson, disguised in feminine attire, began to seek out subversives in Toronto's more stylish bars and clubs, bohemian coffee rooms, jazz cellars, and parks. Jock was, to begin with, uncomfortable, even awkward, in his new role. But it wasn't long before he learned to answer to his code name – Jane – with a bewitching toss of his gorgeous blonde wig. There were compensations too. Long used to leaky tents, sleeping bags, and the itch of Penman's long winter woollies, he understandably came to adore his new silk lingerie, lacy panties, cashmeres, shantungs, nylons and – above all – his candy-striped pink sheets. No doubt about it. Arpège smelled sweeter than Mantan, Lanvin was easier on the skin than Snap, and it was nice to have others pay for your drinks, open doors for you, and sometimes even whistle as you passed. Only one thing bothered Jock. He had decided to join the RCMP after he had seen Gary Cooper in *Northwest Mounted Police* and somehow it was difficult for him to reconcile his present mission with the initial inspiration.

Something else. Jock's first weeks as Jane were characterized by failure.

The first Tuesday, for instance, all Jock could report to the Colonel was the name and badge number of a metro policewoman who had tried to seduce him. The next Tuesday – hopeful, excited, proud – Jock told the Colonel how he had encountered the famous Seymour Bone in a bar, slyly led him on, and got the ruffian to admit that there was much to admire in Russia.

'Hm.' The Colonel went to the cabinet marked LUNATIC FRINGE and dug out the Bone dossier. 'Did he tell you that he can't get into the States? They're afraid to let him in?'

Jock nodded.

'They'd let him in all right. Truth is he's afraid to go there. Here he's Mr Big, there he's unknown. Too much competition for him there, I suppose.'

Next week's revelation didn't come to much, either.

'It's not merely that Snipes got fresh with me, I'm getting used to that, even from married men,' Jock said, tugging at his skirt, 'but he wanted me to try a pill. Morphine. And he showed me the needle he always carries with him, if and when he wants to main-line it.'

'Oh, Snipes. A very publicity-conscious little fellow. The pills are really aspirins and, as for the needle, well the poor man's a diabetic.'

Then it happened, the worst, Jock fell, as they say, head over heels in love.

One gloriously sunny afternoon he thought that he would go for a stroll on the University of Toronto campus and perhaps investigate a student or two. It was not only that these youngsters were less likely to be bald, shorter than he was, and suffer from bad breath, but he had heard that some of the lads had come under the influence of a particularly odious pinko professor. Norman Gore. Anyway that's where Jock first saw him . . . the boy.

He sat alone on a bench, creamy-faced, cheeks flushed, eyes radiating innocence and melancholy. Jock, heart thumping, resorted to the oldest ploy: he dropped his handkerchief.

'Miss ?'

So they fell to talking. The boy, called Jim, was surprisingly full of sharp questions. He wanted to know all about Jane and, again and again, Jock had to fend him off with coy, evasive answers. Finally, mindful of his duty to be done, Jock said,

'See you have a book there. Have you ever, I wonder, read anything by . . . em, Howard Fast?'

Please, no, he thought. Not this innocent lad.

'Yes.'

'Do you admire the singing of . . . em, Paul Robeson?'

'Yes. You?'

'Immensely,' Jock said, ashamed that it was his mission to lead the lad on; stricken, because it was his duty to probe, discover, and, ultimately, report. So upset, in fact, that no sooner did Jock open the door to his apartment than he burst into tears. He had arranged to meet the lad again, the following day, and one part of Jock planned not to turn up (he had, as yet, filed no report on Jim), but another, older Jock reminded him that it was his duty. Something else. He simply couldn't wait to see Jim again. He'd wear his little Simonetta number. Just the thing.

Yes it was.

For the next afternoon, even as they chatted heatedly about Marx, Mao, and others, Jock and Jim held hands. The following evening in the park they kissed for the first time.

On Tuesday Col Smith-Williams asked, 'Anything to report, dear?'

'Nothing,' Jock said, lowering his eyes.

Again and again Jock struggled not to keep his daily rendezvous with Jim, but he was driven to the lad, he couldn't keep away from him. Even more horrifying to Jock was the realization that Jim had fallen for him: the lad was madly in love with – with Jane. 'You're lovely,' he said, 'so lovely, Jane. You ought to be in films.'

'It was once my dream,' Jock confessed. (Actually, he had hoped to be another Bogart, but how to explain it?)

'You must give me your photograph,' Jim said.

'Why?'

'I have connections. Maybe I can do something for you.'

Oh, sweet lad. Jock was touched. He allowed himself to be kissed and caressed.

'Jane. My darling Jane.'

Oh, God, forgive me.

That night as he shaved, that night as Sgt Jock Wilson looked his reflection full in the face, he thought, you swine, you unspeakable swine. Would his name end up on that infamous roll of those who had dishonoured the force? There were already many, too many, on the force who had, so to speak, been hoisted by their own petard. Conners, sent out to crack a heroin ring, had ended up as a pusher. Manley, once the intellectual pride of HQ, had decided to bone up on Marx before joining the CP under a cover-name: today he did that scandalous weekly broadcast to Canada from Moscow. And Seeley. Seeley had taken years, deliciously long years, to smash the white slave traffic in Vancouver. Damn it, Jock thought, it's not *my* soul I'm worried about – and it was true. It was Jim, his Jim, who concerned him so. The lad thinks he's fallen for a luscious doll. (One must remain objective, Jock thought, I'm certainly not a bag.) What happens when he finds out what I am? Done for. His life ruined. I mustn't see him again, Jock thought. Be it treason, I must avoid the lad.

Sometimes, Jock dared to think, a country can ask too much of a man.

And yet, and yet, he would see Jim once more. If only to persuade the lad to give up smoking. Jim favoured little cigars. Dutch they were. Schimmelpennincks.

7

Professor Gore seemed so upset Atuk could hardly refuse to see him. 'Come in,' he said. 'Come in.'

'I'm so glad you found time for me, Atuk, before . . .' Gore had to chuckle. '. . . "before the sun sunk into the ice-blue . . ."'

Atuk recognized the quotation and winced. He replied, '. . . "and black sky was enemy to hunter hungering for home" . . .'

'It's still one of my favourites.'

'Your translation was brilliant,' Atuk said.

'Atuk, I'm glad to hear your heart is still with the Muse. I came to see you because I've heard so many nasty rumours recently.'

'Oh?'

'This office of yours. Rory Peel . . . Snipes . . .'

'A man has to earn a living,' Atuk said.

'But can it be true you're lending your name to products for Twentyman? Esky-Products. I mean you know that he is one of the biggest shareholders in the company that exploits your people.'

'I do not know.'

A pause.

'Men with greased words come here and ask me to sign little papers. I am grateful for Toronto's goodness to me. They give me money. I sign. I am able to send money to the Bay to fight my people's hunger and sickness. Is that bad, Professor?'

'They are shrewd schemers, Atuk, and you must beware of them.'

'Oh. Good you tell me so.'

'To these men you are not a noble savage, a thing of beauty, but something else to exploit and murder. Maybe we can still do something about it. Bring the papers you've signed to my house. We'll go over them together.'

'As you say, Professor. For I loathe the Twentyman, enemy of our people.'

Gore left at last.

I wish that square would stop bugging me, Atuk thought.

Gore was too upset to attend today's faculty meeting at Eglinton. So he phoned, offering his apologies, and went straight home instead.

'Yoo-hoo!'

No answer.

'Nancy?'

'Cripes!' Nancy hurried into the living-room in her kimono. 'I wasn't expecting you back until this evening.'

'I decided to cut the faculty meeting. I'm not feeling well. I – *Good God, who are you?*'

'Him, dearest?'

'Amos de winda cleana, boss.'

'Haven't I seen you somewhere before?'

'No suh,' the tall, muscular Negro said. 'Well, dat will be all of five fishbacks, m'am.'

Gore gave him the money. He went into the bedroom, sat down on the bed, and took off his shoes. Everywhere he turned he was greeted by variations of his own image.

'I had him polish all the mirrors while he was here,' Nancy said. 'You'd think he might have put them back in place, wouldn't you?'

'I'm sure I've seen that fellow before.'

'You couldn't have.'

'Oh, I know. He cleans windows for the Bones too. That's where I saw him.'

'Ruthy Bone? *He certainly does not.*'

'Sorry, dearest. That's where I saw him.'

Nancy had begun to sob. 'It's not true,' she said. 'He doesn't clean windows for Ruthy too.'

Gore stared down at her thoughtfully, troubled. 'I would have thought,' he said, 'you'd be pleased that a coloured man was getting so much work.'

But Nancy was inconsolable.

8

'Old One.' Atuk loathed addressing him like that, but ever since his father had figured in that prize-winning National Film Board short he had insisted on it. 'Old One,' Atuk continued, 'I have found the girl I want to marry.'

'Is she a nice Eskimo girl?'

Atuk scratched the back of his neck.

'Speak no more. Atuk, my son, I remember when your eyes were deep and true as the blue spring sea. I recall when your soul was pure and white as the noon iceberg. This is no more. Today—'

'For Christ's sake, will you cut out that crazy talk. You sound like you were auditioning for Disney again or something.'

'If not for the fact that I was taller than John Mills—'

'All right. I'm not saying you shouldn't have had the part. But—'

'I do not wish to hear of marriage with a non-Eskimo girl.'

'You know something, Old One. You're a bigot. You've never overcome your igloo mentality.'

'I'm proud of my heritage.'

83

'So am I. Only I refuse to be imprisoned by it.'

'Tell me, Atuk. What would you do about the children?'

He didn't reply.

'How would it be for me to sit your little half-breed on my lap and he wouldn't be able to speak an Eskimo word?'

'We've discussed the question of children. We intend to give them a modern type education.'

'Ha! But will his friends at school let him forget he is an Eskimo? Atuk. Atuk, harken to me.'

'Won't you even meet the girl? I love her.'

'Shall I go to their home. To be stared at. An Eskimo. Would I feel relaxed there, Atuk? I'd have to wash and eat with cutlery. Do they know the joys of smoked deer meat? Minced seal pancakes? No. I'd be expected to eat condemned foods. Like filet mignon.'

'So you'd make a few adjustments. A big deal.'

The Old One gave Atuk a savage look. He sighed deeply. 'It all begins with taking a bath. It seems a little compromise, I know. But one day you take a bath and the next you have turned your back on your own people. Now I suppose,' he added contemptuously, 'it is nothing for you to eat fish that has been cooked?'

'There are other problems besides the Eskimo problem, Old One. I am a man who just happens to be an Eskimo.'

'You can stand there and tell me that when you

know as I do that before the great ice-sheet drew back this land was ours from sea to sea.'

'Let's face the facts. We're never getting the land back.'

'Atuk, you have a good Eskimo head on your shoulders. Think. They believe in pills and *artificially* frozen foods. How could you ever feel at home in such a background?'

'I'm not marrying a background. I'm marrying the girl I love.'

'Ignak is right. An Eskimo who lives away from his land is no Eskimo.'

'Ignak is an Eskimo fascist. OK. Don't say it. It all starts with taking a bath.'

'Go, marry. But you have not got your father's blessing.'

'She's a fine girl, Old One. Very fat and oily. Stinky too. Like one of ours. Won't you even meet her?'

'Tell me, what would she say, for instance, if you wanted to hunt next Saturday?'

'Well, as a matter of fact, Saturday wouldn't do. It's their day of rest.'

The Old One looked baffled.

'You see, their God . . . em, created the world in six days,' Atuk said in a faltering voice, 'and on the seventh day, Saturday, he rested.'

'Oh,' the Old One said, slapping his knee, 'it's one of those one-God religions, is it?'

'*So what?*'

'Through all the ages, from the time of the great ice-sheet, what has held our people together? Speak!'

'Our belief in plenty of gods.'

'We are the chosen pagans, my son. We have a message for the world.'

'You live in the past, Old One. The ice is never coming back. Our people will never again hunt the white bear in the Bay of San Francisco or run dog-sled races in Miami.'

'It is written that—'

'I don't care what's written.'

'No. You think it's poetry, that's all. Good reading.' The Old One paused for breath. 'What would she say, Atuk, if you wanted to eat smoked caribou? Remember the caribou sandwiches after the hunt at Benny's? With blubber on the side?'

Atuk grinned.

'Well, what would she say?'

'Deer is out. It's unclean.'

'*What?*'

'You see, in this particular branch of one-god religions—'

'What is it called?'

'It's called the Jews. The Hebrews.'

'Are they Jews or Hebrews?'

'It depends on their income. The poor ones are Jews.'

'Jews, Christians, Hebrews. I'm not concerned with nuances. They're all white. Atuk, it's hard to

86

be an Eskimo. I told you so long ago. But you must hold your head high. Why, in this country when it comes to culture what is there besides the Eskimo? Our sculpture is acclaimed the world over. Our poetry too. And one day we shall rise again and claim the land that is rightly ours . . . from sea to sea, as it is written . . .'

Atuk lowered his head.

'Return with me to Baffin Bay. Tonight.'

'No. Never. What is there for me at the Bay? Disney shoots about one picture every two years and the Film Board pays nigger wages. Shall I be like Kupi? Can you see me building a block of igloos with inferior ice and soaking my tribe for it? I'm going to marry the girl and settle here.'

'You think you've been accepted, don't you? Ha!' The Old One grinned spitefully. 'Tell me, Atuk, will you be obliged to use the missionary position?'

'That's none of your goddam business!'

'For the rest of your life—' he gasped, shaking with laughter. 'For – the miss—' Again, it was too much. 'The miss – missionary position.'

Laughter came from the hall too. The giggling of girls.

'Oh, that's rich! What fun! The miss—'

Everyone but Ignak scattered when Atuk opened the door.

'Assimilationist!'

Atuk pushed him aside.

'But you will be getting what you deserve very

soon,' Ignak called after him, 'or haven't you seen today's headlines?'

Atuk poured himself a stiff drink. Afterwards he didn't bathe, even though it was the tenth day of the month and he had promised himself, as a matter of personal discipline, to bathe at least once a month. She will have to take me as I am, he thought. An Eskimo. No more missionary position.

9

Bette was trying to do something about this week's accumulation of fan mail. There were the usual requests. A librarian from Moncton, NB, had sent a stick of Wrigley's gum for her to chew and return (a self-addressed envelope was enclosed). There were at least thirty photographs to sign. A member of the British Columbia legislature asked Bette if she would be good enough to wear high button shoes on her next television appearance and a persistent fan from Montreal asked once more for her soiled nylons. Bette, making a note to return the man's cheque again, shook her head, and wondered whether the fool didn't know he could buy nylons, *new* nylons, for less money. Her self-elected aunt, in Moose Jaw, Sask., had written a sweet letter and Mr O'Toole, absolutely Bette's favourite, had sent a cigarette box he had made himself. There were still more requests for photographs.

Bette gave up.

She knew Atuk's show had been taped days in advance and Atuk had promised, he had given his word, that he would come to watch it with her. He had promised to be there promptly at six and here it was eight o'clock and he still hadn't arrived.

Bette simply couldn't sit still. She tried the parallel bars, but that didn't work. Neither did the bicycle machine or the punching bag. She seemed to be driven by a surfeit of energy, an edginess she just couldn't work off. Bette couldn't understand it. Even swimming hardly pleased her any more. Nothing, in fact, satisfied like giving help. I guess, she thought, reaching for the gin bottle again, it's like I'm a nun. Sort of. If only Atuk needed help more often, she thought, like in the old days. The good old days.

Was it possible, just possible, that Goldie was giving him help now? *No.*

Bette lit a cigarette, put it out quickly, and reached for the gin and carrot juice. She phoned Atuk once more. No answer. 'Goddam him,' she said aloud.

Well, time for the show. Bette sat down before the television set, filing her nails, and switched to *Crossed Swords* with Seymour Bone.

The massive redhead faded in with a bucolic smile. 'The programme,' he said, 'is *Crossed Swords* and the rules are very simple. Viewers send in a controversial quotation and our panel of experts tries to identify the quotation and then discusses it. Our guests tonight, ladies and gentlemen, are Rabbi Glenn Seigal, Harry Snipes, Canada's Angriest Young Editor, Rory Peel, advertising executive and Atuk, the poet. Gentlemen, our first quotation.'

A card flashed before the camera.

BLESSED ARE THE MEEK: FOR THEY SHALL INHERIT THE EARTH

The panel looked pensive.

'He was born in humble circumstances,' Bone said. 'His father practised one of the graphic arts.'

'Hemingway,' Snipes said. 'I recognize the style.'

'Not a bad guess. You might say he influenced Hemingway.' Bone turned to the viewers with a twinkle in his eye. 'And many others too. An under-privileged child, you might say he developed into an excitable, malajusted adolescent.'

'Not one of the Angry Young Men,' Rabbi Seigal said.

'Well, of his time perhaps.' Bone couldn't resist a chuckle. 'To go back even earlier, the conditions of his birth, well, this is the CBC and it's not our policy to take sides on matters like these but, ah, I might venture, I think I might safely venture that the conditions of his birth were allegedly unique. He was purported to have magical gifts. He, ah, per-formed a world-famous feat with fish.'

Obviously, they were still stumped.

'Atuk. Haven't *you* any ideas?'

'No.'

'One more hint, then. He was a religious leader ... a widely-quoted author ... *still* a best-seller ...'

'Herman Wouk!'

'Sorry, no.'

Rabbi Seigal looked embarrassed. 'I try to read all the important books as they come out, but, well, it's impossible to keep up with everything. Hardly any time to read for pleasure any more ...'

'All right. *Another hint.* He died at an early age under unnatural, even cruel conditions. Well, Atuk?'

Atuk shrugged.

'Gentlemen?'

'I've got it,' Snipes said. *'Chessman. Carl Chessman.'*

'Nope.'

'What's that Russian,' Rory Peel demanded, excited, 'he wrote the property that won the Nobel Prize. He's got a name like black bread.'

'Pumpernickel?'

'Pasternak!'

'Nope. Gentlemen,' Bone said, 'enough. Now let's turn to the merit of the thought itself. "Blessed are the meek: for they shall inherit the earth." Mr Peel?'

'Well, Seymour, I'd like to see some statistics before I commit myself, but speaking off the top of my head, well, no.'

'Atuk? Haven't you *anything* to say?'

91

'The thought is inspiring, much inspiring, but where has it got my people?'

'Mr Snipes?'

'That's just the kind of namby-pamby talk that leads to welfare statism and' – he turned menacingly towards Rabbi Seigal – 'and pacifism. Or to put a true label on it, selling your country down the river. It—'

'—it's not the sort of sentiment that built this great country out of a wilderness,' Rory Peel said.

'And,' Rabbi Seigal said, '*and* perpetuated needless cruelties against the original Canadians: the Eskimo.'

Atuk blew his nose.

'You don't *stand* anywhere on nuclear disarmament, Rabbi,' Snipes said. 'You're on your knees.'

'Look here, I—'

'Order,' Bone said. 'Order. Rabbi?'

'When you take the thought inherent in the quotation under discussion and analyse it purely as a religious slogan, well, it lacks the impact of – The Family That Prays Together Stays Together. The quotation, I believe, runs, Blessed are the meek for they shall inherit the earth. Well, speaking professionally, this lacks appeal. Nobody today wants to be thought of as weak, a shmo, if you'll pardon me. We like to think of ourselves as lions.'

The doorbell rang. At last, Bette thought, and she started to unzip her skirt with one hand and undo her blouse buttons with the other. But it wasn't Atuk.

'Doc Burt!'

'Himself. Back from the hills at last.'

'Sorry,' she said, 'I only had time to slip into these things when the bell rang.'

'Your young feller here?'

'No.'

He didn't seem at all surprised.

'But he promised he was coming. I have no idea what's keeping him.'

'Sure, sure. Well I wanted to have a private little pow-wow with you anyway.'

Bette turned down the sound on the set and tottered over to the table and fixed two gin and carrot juices.

'It's about the sort of help you're giving the Eskimo.'

At the very mention of the subject Bette felt parched, edgy again. Like she had to scratch herself everywhere.

'You don't approve?'

'On the contrary. I think it's wonderful of you. I'm proud.'

'Oh, Doc,' she said, sitting down beside him on the sofa, 'I knew you'd understand.'

'Why, I've known you since you were this high,' he said, pressing his hairy hand against her thigh. 'Never was a purer, cleaner-minded girl born in the province.'

Bette blushed.

'Come closer, child. Let ole Doc Burt help you with your buttons.'

Until he mentioned it, Bette hadn't realized that two buttons had still been left undone. Head thrust back, she leaned forward tenderly. Dr Parks caressed her throat with one hand and, with the other, fumbled and fussed with the buttons. 'How I admire your lung-power,' he said.

He was not, to Bette's astonishment, all that fatherly about it. In fact, it seemed to Bette that he was squeezing her breasts.

'You have the most lovely pectorals too.'

The room began to spin.

'Remember how you used to sit on my lap?'

'Mm-hm.'

'Would you do it again, for a sentimental ole fool?'

Bette climbed gracefully on to his lap and the edginess that had bothered her before seemed all-consuming now. Doc Burt told her about his troubles. 'We had to disband the troupe in Moose Jaw.' Brotherly love, Doc Burt discovered, had gone too far between Best Developed Biceps of Sunnyside Beach and Lake Ontario Jr. The boys were arrested on a morality charge. 'It was terrible,' Doc Burt said, 'just terrible.' Bette felt a hand start under her skirt. 'But I managed to get the boys paroled under my custody and things have taken a turn for the better since.' Doc Burt told her that he had been made manager of this year's Miss Canada contest. With his free hand, he reached into his inside jacket pocket and showed Bette photographs of some of the more promising competitors. One of them was a striking, unusually tall blonde. Jane Something. 'And do you know what,' Doc Burt continued, 'Jean-Paul McEwen has agreed to be one of the judges.'

Bette squirmed as the Doc's hand ventured higher. She drew his head compulsively to her bosom.

'Bette, a word from the wise. The thing about giving help is that once you start there's simply no end to it.'

'Uh-huh,' she said, 'uh-huh,' vaguely conscious of her stockings being rolled down so slowly she had to suppress a cry.

'It's just give, give, give.'

Her eyes shut, Bette nodded.

'Not that your Eskimo fellow would care. He's getting help elsewhere these days.'

That did it. Bette leaped up. 'Is he? Honestly? Why, isn't that just wonderful!'

'You mean you're not jealous?'

'But, Doc. You don't understand. It's like I was Sister Kenny and my first patient had just learned to walk.'

'You mean to say there are, um, other patients?'

'Now, now. Mustn't pry.' As Bette turned to do up her stockings she was startled to see Seymour

Bone watching her. 'Could you at least turn off the set, Doc.'

Dr Parks turned up the sound in error. Bone's image was cut off in mid-sentence. 'We interrupt this programme to bring you a special bulletin. The RCMP, working in close co-operation with the FBI, has uncovered an important clue in the search for the missing Colonel Swiggert of the US Air Force. The Colonel's—'

Bette switched off the set herself. Atuk's heading for trouble, she thought. Bad trouble. He's going to need a powerful friend. Bette picked up the phone and dialled Twentyman's unlisted number.

10

Atuk, nobody's fool, had already purchased two aeroplane tickets to London under the pseudonyms Mr and Mrs Chong. Laden down with parcels, he pounded on the door to his house. 'Hey!' It was Ti-Lucy, to his surprise, who undid the locks one by one and lifted the bar for him.

'Where's the Old One?' Atuk asked, immediately suspicious.

'All is not well, brother. You'd better come down to the basement.'

'Let's see today's figures,' Atuk asked quickly.

Ti-Lucy handed him her clip-board with the production figures. 'But that's not bad,' Atuk said.

'You'd better come down to the basement.'

Atuk had a look at the day's output. Every painting was representative. Literal. The statues were perfectly shaped. All crudeness and innocence gone. 'For Christ's sake,' Atuk said, ripping a painting in two, 'if I want Norman Rockwell quality goods I can hire Rockwell.'

Brothers, sisters, cousins, aunts and uncles, all tried to conceal themselves behind the thrusting, bellicose figure of Ignak.

'I should have guessed you were behind this. Well, speak up.'

'Why is it,' Ignak asked, 'you always want us to paint and sculpt badly?'

'That's what they want, not me.'

'We refuse to be condescended to,' Ignak said.

The others nodded in agreement.

'Gratitude. There's gratitude for you.' Atuk picked up a statue. 'Even if I had Souvenir of Niagara Falls stamped on the back of this it would only bring in two–three cents apiece.' He heaved the statue against the wall, breaking it. 'They make this crap better in Japan.'

'What's wrong with our brothers, the Japanese?' Ignak demanded.

Atuk groaned.

'We wish,' Ignak said, 'you would remember Baffin Bay and how the white scum rule our land.'

'How long will you hold a grudge? Another thousand years?'

'The Japanese believe in Asia for the Asians. We believe in America for the Americans,' Ignak said.

Atuk sighed. 'Better get me a Scotch, Ti-Lucy. With lotsa ice.'

'Right away.'

'OK,' Atuk continued, 'we'll treat this as a bad joke. Ill-advised. Throw today's junk into the garbage and get back to work. Make me some stuff I can sell.'

But nobody moved.

'We want an equal share in the profits,' Ignak said.

'The what? Who feeds and protects you? Profits? You're crazy, man.'

'They know about the many boxes with the coloured papers in them,' Ti-Lucy said. 'You know, the ones with the Queen's pictures and the numbers on them.'

'Ah ha.'

'You have lied to us about many things,' Mush-Mush said resentfully.

'It is a falsehood about the magic box.'

Only then did Atuk notice that the television set had been taken apart.

'It is not filled with little spirits waiting for your command.'

'Too bad about the magic box,' Atuk said, accepting another drink. 'There was a blockbuster movie on tonight. The Bogart.'

'Oh!'

'Gee whiz!'

'Tell you what,' Atuk said, 'you ask Mr Big here. He'll make the magic box work for you again.'

All eyes were turned on Ignak.

'Don't let him sway you. Remember—'

'But the Bogart, Ignak.'

'All these boxes you see here,' Atuk said, 'are filled with gifts. I risked my life on the outside this morning so that I could bring my loyal, hard-working family surprises. A doll for Big Annie. A giant-size bottle of Parker's Ink for Loo-Loo, an electric train for Mush-Mush and for Moose, the new *Playboy* calendar . . .'

Moose rolled over on the floor and began to whine. The others surged forward.

'Wait,' Ignak said. 'Do you want his trinkets, his imperialist baubles, or do you want equal shares?'

Nobody knew what to say.

'Ask him why he locks us in here?' Ignak said.

'I don't lock you in here. *I keep them out.* Have you any idea what goes on outside? Rape. Murder. Robbery.'

'He lies,' Ignak said.

'OK,' Atuk said, 'I'll tell you what. Ti-Lucy, bring me a box of papers with the Queen's pictures.'

Atuk emptied the box on the floor, fifty dollar bills scattering everywhere. 'Take,' he shouted. 'Help yourself.'

Nobody dared.

'Can you eat those papers?' Atuk asked. 'No. Can

you make of them electric trains? Frozen fish? Magic boxes? No, no, no. I happen to collect them. It's my weakness. With some people it's book-matches and with me it's—'

'They are used for trading,' Ignak insisted. 'They are very valuable.'

Atuk burst out laughing. 'He's for the flip-factory. Here, Choy, take one. Would you give me a sack of potatoes for this? Look at the picture.'

The fifty-dollar bill was passed from hand to hand.

'Atuk's right. She's not very pretty.'

'Hardly worth a sack of potatoes.'

'I would be willing to offer more,' Mush-Mush said, 'for Miss September of the *Playboy*.'

'How about Miss March?'

Suddenly Moose stepped forward. 'Maybe you are right about the outside, Atuk, and you are truly brave to venture there.'

'He lies,' Ignak shouted.

'But inside we never have girls.'

'We are lonely.'

'We want boom-boom.'

'That's right,' Mush-Mush said, 'for it is never the same with your sister.'

Ti-Lucy flushed. Big Annie began to crawl under a bed.

'Oh, you filthy swine,' Atuk said. 'You pigs! Primitives! I ought to whip the lot of you.'

'You see,' Ignak said, 'he has turned against us.'

'You want chicks,' Atuk said. 'I'll get you chicks.'

'Yowie!'

'Atta boy!'

'Don't be swayed. He tricks you.'

'You're beginning to sound like a broken record, Ignak. Besides, you boys may want girls, but we all know what Ignak craves.'

The boys began to giggle. Choy stepped forward. 'But I would like one too,' he said.

'You filthy things, that's not allowed here.'

'I'm not asking for myself,' Ignak said. 'Only for Choy's sake.'

'Sure, darling. You bet.'

The boys began to whoop it up. Mush-Mush wet a finger and stroked his eyebrow. Moose tried to sit on Ignak's lap, but he was given a shove.

'You are being swayed by cheap promises,' Ignak said. 'He lies through his teeth.' Then he fled the room.

'Now back to work,' Atuk said, 'the lot of you.'

'Will you make us another magic box?'

'You get the lead out of your ass,' Atuk said, starting up the stairs, 'and turn in some work I can use and I'll get you another box.'

The phone rang. Rang again. Ti-Lucy took it. 'It's a Mr Twentyman,' she said. 'He wishes to speak to you urgently.'

11

Jean-Paul McEwen, the most fearless columnist in Toronto, leaned back in her swivel chair and wondered what she could possibly expose today. The squalor of restaurant kitchens was out and she had already broken a store window and done thirty days to tell the truth about prison conditions. Not enough time had elapsed since her last advertising exposé column (the claims, the facts) for her to do another. Maybe she ought to try living on an old age pensioner's allowance for a month. Naw; she was too old for that kind of job.

Jean-Paul McEwen looked at her watch. She was waiting for her field operators to report on her racial prejudice survey. It had been one hell of a dull week, actually. Nobody had socked her on the jaw. McEwen studied the work charts on her wall glumly. She was behind with her minutorials (sixty second opinion capsules broadcast every hour on Station CFTK) and she hadn't one good idea in mind for her weekly television show.

Son-of-a-bitch.

A half hour passed and McEwen still sat inertly at her desk. Another hour went by without a word written or a dime earned. Worse. While she sat there, like an idiot, other columnists were getting ahead, her house was depreciating, and her peak years were passing. The rat-race. She could do a column on how glad she was to be a Canadian and out of the US-style rat-race. Naw. Old hat. McEwen felt wretched because she was not a woman to waste time. A quarrel with her mother ended up as a thought-piece on parenthood and the letters she got about the column made for a humorous minutorial on Letters I Get. Everywhere Jean-Paul McEwen went she took her tape recorder. You never knew who might say something useful or where you might come up with a honey of an idea. Even McEwen's vacations were not a costly waste. The funny things that happened to her were worth at least three columns. She published the bedtime stories. she made up for her nieces as a book. But today McEwen was stuck.

Stuck?

Jean-Paul McEwen was sitting on a bomb, the biggest story of her career, and she couldn't do anything about it. McEwen was in love.

Years ago when Jean-Paul McEwen, actually born Polly McEwen, decided to become a reporter, she resolved to take a man's name – for nobody in Canada would take a woman columnist seriously – and to sacrifice all personal pleasures or commitments to her pursuit of the truth. No marriage, no family. Modelling herself on Lincoln Steffens, the girl had, as a matter of fact, done much to expose the shame of at least one city; and not one of her enemies could accuse her of bribe-taking or favouritism. But now, now there was Jane.

What happened was that one day one of Jean-Paul McEwen's many, breathless operatives reported that following hard on the new trend toward teenage nightclubs, an enterprising Bulgarian had come up with the idea of call-girls for the under twenty set. These girls would be available at cut rates to the twixt teen 'n twenty crowd only during the twilight hours, that is to say, before the adult rush hour. It was not a profitable enterprise *per se*. But like the supermarket sales leader that is sold at cost or, still better, the Junior Bank Account, it was hoped that it help the youngsters acquire a taste that in later, higher income years, they would find hard to give up. Put more succinctly, it appeared that even whoremongers were betting on Canada's future.

Anyway Jean-Paul McEwen, disguised as a student, went out to investigate – and fell in love.

Worse news. To judge from Jane's behaviour, the scheme was even more horrific than Jean-Paul had suspected.

—Have you read Howard Fast? Do you admire the singing of Paul Robeson?

It was not only bodily corruption the Bulgarian's girls were bent on, they had been trained to seduce the minds of Young Canada as well.

Yet though McEwen already had sufficient data with which to impale Jane in the court of public opinion the truth was she had still to write a word and, to put it bluntly, close her case by taking Jane to bed. But how could she? Goddam it. You struggled, you worked, you won prizes and, you dared to hope, acceptance, but in the end it was still a man's world. We have been appeased, we have been mollified, but no more. They gave us the vote, equal pay in *some* industries, liberating appliances for the home, seats in government, and then they stop short. For some jobs it was still Men Only.

Son-of-a-bitch.

McEwen had to face an even more unpleasant truth. Even if I could, would I? No. I'm in love. I adore her.

Enough, she thought. There's work to be done.

McEwen lit up a Schimmelpenninck, opened the bottom drawer of her desk, and pulled out her list of Just-So Ideas, when the first of her field operators burst into the room.

Selby ripped off his false Jimmy Durante-type nose and removed his flashy tie. 'No go,' he said, disheartened. 'I did just as you asked. I walked up to the reservation desk. I told them my name was Hymie Bercovitch. I insisted on a room overlooking the lake, and what do you know? OK, sir, the guy says.'

'Don't tell me,' McEwen said, 'you didn't remember to pick your nose.'

'I did everything you rehearsed with me. I bargained until I was blue in the face, and guess what?

They knocked twenty bucks off the price of my reservation, that's what.'

'Do you realize that I'm now stuck with two reservations at that hotel? One under the name of Smith and the other under Bercovitch?'

'But I tried everything I could to get them to insult me, Jean-Paul. I guess your information was wrong or it's a lousy season and they'll take anybody. The guy at the desk even said to me, "Some of my best friends are Jews." '

'But that's an anti-Semitic remark,' McEwen said. 'Did you hit him?'

'Gee, I'm sorry, Jean-Paul. I thought he was being nice.'

The next to report was Bell, still in blackface. His forehead was bandaged. 'They wouldn't serve you,' McEwen said happily. 'There was an incident.'

'Wouldn't serve me? Hell, I've only been able to afford the Roof Garden five times before in my life and each time I got a table by the kitchen door. This time nothing but ringside. I've never had such service in my life!' Bell banged his broad-brimmed fedora angrily against the desk. 'Last week the ambassador from Ghana was there and left everybody enormous tips.'

'But you were in a fight. What happened?'

'Well, after I left there I was so depressed I went to the Plaza to knock back a couple of short ones. Well you know, I forgot I had this stuff on my face. George – you know, the coloured waiter, he's been serving me every day for years, well, George comes over and I say, "Get me a double scotch. But quick," and the next thing I know he's lifted me up by the collar and he's shaking me. "I have to take that sort of bull from all the ofay trash here," he says. "From you I expect please. Out, boy." And he kicks me down the steps.'

McEwen didn't comment.

'When they were sitting-in down south I bought George a drink. The night Patterson took the Swede I congratulated him. I thought George loved me but he's hated me all these years because I'm white.' A tear welled in Bell's eye. 'He's prejudiced, Jean-Paul.'

The last field operator to report was Arnold. 'Oh, I've got a hot one,' he said, immensely pleased with himself. 'Boy, have I ever got a lulu.'

'Yeah?'

'What if I told you that Bette Dolan has been picking up guys in the bar at the King Edward?'

'Simple. I'd fire you for drinking.'

'Well it happens to be God's truth.'

McEwen laughed in his face. 'Ever since that girl swam the lake,' she said, 'and turned down all the money she could have had out of TV endorsements, I've had my eye on her. She's incorruptible, Arnold. The McCoy. She *does* give most of her money away to charity. She's a good girl.'

'Maybe all that has changed since she got involved with the Eskimo jerk.'

'Look, everybody's tried to make Bette. Don't tell me Atuk, of all unlikely people—'

'All right. *You* go to the King Edward. She usually comes in around nine. What you do, see, is tell her you need help.'

'Nonsense.'

'Go ahead, Jean-Paul. Try.'

But McEwen had another, more shameful rendezvous to keep. As soon as her operatives had left she changed into her other clothes. She became, so to speak, Jim.

'Darling.'

'Yes,' Jock said.

'I have the most wonderful news for you.'

'Really?'

'Remember the photograph you gave me? Well, I entered it in the Miss Canada contest. Jane, *you're one of the finalists*!'

'Christ Almighty!'

'Aren't you pleased?'

'What will my poor old mother say?'

'There's nothing immodest about it. Why, I'll bet you she'll be pleased. This may be your first step to stardom.'

12

It was just one of those days for Atuk. Dreadful. Simply dreadful. The Old One didn't come down for breakfast again.

'You know what he's doing upstairs in his room?' Ignak asked. 'Praying for his dead son. You.'

Moose tip-toed into the dining-room, followed by Mush-Mush.

'Which one of you stole my ascot last night?'

Actually, Atuk was pleased that at least one of the boys had enough taste to dress up for a girl.

'But we had to have something to gag her with for she screamed so loud.'

'Loud*ly*. Why'd she scream?'

'Well, you see, we had to tie her to the bed.'

'Oh, no.'

'But you didn't tell her there would be eight of us, brother.'

'You go upstairs and cut that girl free this minute.'

The brothers started resentfully out of the room.

'And you want them to run the whole country again,' Atuk said to Ignak. 'They're savages.'

Ignak held up the morning paper triumphantly and watched for Atuk's reaction to the headlines. 'Speaking of savages,' he said, 'you may have some fast talking to do yourself soon.'

'I'm not worried.'

But Atuk gulped down his coffee and drove straight to Twentyman's office.

Bette Dolan had been to see Twentyman. She had spilled the beans. But Twentyman, to Atuk's surprise, spoke quietly. He did not seem angry, but hurt.

'Why,' Twentyman asked, 'didn't you tell me about this – about your part in it – before?'

'I thought it best not to.'

'I suppose you're ready to flee the country.'

Atuk had to admit it was true.

'Fool!'

'Now look here—'

Twentyman began to laugh. 'Oh, you little fool. Just when you've got it made.'

Twentyman then outlined his amazing plans to Atuk.

'But it sounds very risky to me,' Atuk said.

'Not at all,' Twentyman said. 'As long as the story proper doesn't break too soon. That much is vital, Atuk. I must have until next Tuesday to get all the spontaneous sectors of our response properly organized.'

'I will see that it is so, then.'

'Jumpy?'

'A little.'

'What about your family?'

'They can be counted on to keep quiet.'

'But why take unnecessary chances? I wish you'd

send them home, Atuk. I could charter a plane for them.'

'My family stays with me.'

'You're too sentimental. Like me. But I admire that in a man.'

'It's just that I cherish my family. Like I stand with Schweitzer. I understand my little brothers and I wish to protect them.'

'What about Sgt Jock Wilson? He's in town, you know.'

'I'll handle him,' Atuk said. 'Don't worry.' Atuk paused at the door. 'Oh, what's all this STICK OUT YOUR NECK stuff? I see signs, billboards, everywhere.'

'I'm glad you asked me that, Atuk. You see you're going to be the first contestant.'

Twentyman explained what was expected of Atuk.

'You're a clever one,' Atuk said.

'We both are.'

Atuk drove to his office to confer with Rory and Miss Stainsby.

'Anything important?' he asked.

'The usual fan mail,' Miss Stainsby said. 'I've booked you to recite at a Haddassah fur show in Montreal. Twenty-fifth of next month. Bette Dolan called again.'

'The bitch. I never want to speak to her again. Oh, before I forget. Make an appointment for me with Rabbi Glenn Seigal.'

'Atuk,' Rory began doubtfully. 'Atuk, I've never interfered before, have I?'

Atuk waited. He knew he and Rory would have to have it out about Goldie one of these days. Why not now?

'Is it true that you agreed with Twentyman earlier this morning to be the first contestant on STICK OUT YOUR NECK?'

'Like that's the story I hear told,' Atuk said, grinning.

'*But do you know the rules?*'

'I sure do. I also know the prize money that's being offered.'

'But, Atuk, what if—'

'I can't lose. Keep this under your hat, Rory, but the whole thing is an elaborate tax dodge. I'm helping Buck over a spot, that's all.'

Rory didn't comment.

'Give,' Atuk said.

'Are you sure you can trust Twentyman?'

'Of course I can't. But come next week he's going to need me more than I need him. In fact he can't do without me, man.'

'He's shrewd. I'd watch him.'

'You watch me. I'm shrewder. Anything else?'

'I understand,' Rory said evenly, 'that you are taking my sister to Professor Gore's for dinner tonight.'

'What if I am?'

'It's hardly a secret,' Rory said, 'that I don't approve.'

'Excuse me,' Miss Stainsby said, fleeing.

'Rory, it's time we had this out, isn't it?'

'I'd say so.'

'You busy for lunch?'

Rory was speaking at a Zionist fund-raising lunch.

'All right, then,' Atuk said. 'Why don't you, Goldie, the Old One and I, meet at the Roof Garden immediately afterwards?'

'If you like,' Rory said, 'but my mind's made up. You must break with my sister.'

'Sure, sure,' Atuk said.

Atuk, held up by a quarrel with the Old One, was late. Yet Goldie was still alone when he finally reached the Roof Garden.

'Hi,' Atuk said, kissing her on the cheek. 'Where's Mr Peel?'

'Like he phoned. He's going to be late.'

'Don't look so worried. We're partners, you know.'

'This is one scene you don't dig. Like he feels it's one thing to do business with you, but another for you to marry his sister.'

'I can handle this.'

'I wish you weren't wearing that suit. Rory's the conservative type.'

'Are you ashamed of me?'

'Certainly not. Sh. Here he comes.'

Atuk jumped up to greet Rory.

'Sorry to be late, but I was tied up at the fund-raising lunch.'

Goldie explained, needlessly, that Rory was one of the most active, dedicated Zionists in Toronto.

'I try to do my bit,' Rory said, 'that's all.'

Atuk ordered drinks all around as the conversation dwindled into a fitful exchange of pleasantries. Goldie laughed too loud at the most inane jokes and Rory was evasive. Nobody dared to be the first to mention what was pressing on all their minds – the question of Rory's approval of their wedding. Atuk began to drink heavily; his manner morose.

Finally, Rory said, 'Where's the, em, Old One?'

'Atuk's had a terrible fight with him,' Goldie said quickly. 'The Old One feels Atuk has turned against his people.'

'There's something to be said for sticking to your own.'

'You don't understand, Rory. I turned against my religion at an early age. Like I'm no *shmock*, you know.'

Rory looked around anxiously to see if anyone had heard a Yiddish word being spoken at his table.

'I'm teaching him the language,' Goldie said.

'Of course, of course. But there's more to a people's tradition than religion. Look at the Hebrews. We took a desert and made a garden out of it.'

'Oh, I admire your people enormously for that.

114

But, speaking for myself, I couldn't swallow that bit about the land being ours by right.'

'Ours,' Rory said charitably, 'but you're not—'

'No. I mean Canada.'

'Canada? Oh,' Rory said. He chuckled, amused. 'You mean to say the Eskimos believe Canada belongs to them?'

'Yeah,' Atuk said, laughing. 'And now there's this group of militant young cats that would like to have it all back. They'd put all you foreigners—'

'I'm Canadian-born. I haven't the least trace of an accent.'

'He didn't mean anything personal.'

'What I meant is that to the Eskimo, to the militants anyway, you're all greenhorns. They'd relocate you all in one province. A sort of national park.'

'But that would be inhuman. Many families have been settled in this country for generations.'

'It's crazy. Like I said. But the land *is* ours by right, you know.'

'Why talk politics,' Goldie said. 'Like—'

'It belonged to our ancestors and—'

'But that was thousands of years ago.'

'Maybe so. But our people have suffered terrible persecutions out on the Bay and—'

'Not from me. I never did harm to an Eskimo—'

'Sure you haven't. It's only the fur hunters and the RCMP. And don't say it, I know. They're good fathers and husbands and the good people of Toronto have no idea what's going on up there. But the fact remains the land is ours and we'd like it back. Some people would, anyway.'

'How amusing. You come back after thousands of years and would like me and my family to move out. Your people sound very aggressive to me.'

'With reason, but. Conditions—'

'One persecution does not excuse another. Just because your people have suffered—'

'It's more than that. The land was promised to us by our gods.'

'Pardon me while I laugh.'

'We have a book. It's all written out there.'

'Look, everybody has a book. This is our country. You can't drive us out like – like Arabs. We're Canadians.'

'To us, you're all Arabs.'

Rory leaped up, knocking over his drink. 'Are you trying to bait me?' he asked.

'Of course not. Sit down, man.'

'Atuk, I'm pleased to have you as a business associate. But you're not ... well, fit to marry into a Jewish family.'

'You don't understand. Jewish, Protestant, you're all white to me.'

Rory gaped. Tears came to his eyes. White. He, Rory Peel, was being called white. This was the compliment, the state of grace, he had striven for all his life. But today, coming from Atuk's mouth, it was delivered as an insult.

'In my opinion, Atuk, you're just a loud, aggressive Eskimo.'

And Rory walked right out of the bar.

'Well, congrats. You said you could handle him and you did. The man from Charmsville.'

'Sorry, baby. But I've been getting it from all sides today.'

'I'll be getting it too. Once Rory gets on the phone to Paw.'

'To hell with it. I will not apologize for what I am. He could have called me anything but an "aggressive Eskimo".' Atuk blew his nose. 'When I used to ski to school as a kid the white boys used to knock me over and beat me up and call me a dirty Eskimo.'

'Oh, my poor darling.'

'I have feelings too, you know. If you prick me, do I not bleed?'

'Ha, ha, ha,' Goldie said. 'Me too, man.'

'I'm a success. A somebody. What do I have to do to prove myself to all the Rorys of this world?'

'I don't care. We'll marry without him.'

'Don't worry. He'll come round. We're still partners, you know. What time is it?'

'Five o'clock.'

'Damn it, we're due at Gore's at six. I'd better go home to change.' Suddenly Atuk laughed. 'Have you ever met his wife?'

'No.'

'She kills me. Nancy goes in for the nose-rubbing bit. Oh, what a night we've got ahead of us.'

13

Once he had changed into his native costume Atuk went down to the basement to dip into the rejects bin for a piece of sculpture he could take to the Gores. He dreaded the polite, goysy evening ahead of him. But there had been a time when he would have been immensely pleased to be invited to the Gores. Atuk, after all, had once been the political hope of his tribe, and Gore had been his mentor in those early days in Toronto.

Ah, when I look back, Atuk thought, lifting his slippered feet on to a hassock and swishing his cigar around in his snifter of Remy Martin. There's nothing to stop me now, is there? No.

Maybe tonight it won't be so bad at Gore's place.

Everybody, but everybody, was going to the buffet dinner at the beloved Professor Gore's. The guest list was so intellectually impressive that one columnist, already invited, observed, 'If the house was hit by a bomb it would blow out the brains of Canada.'

The arts would be represented by Harry Snipes; Bette Dolan could speak for the body beautiful. Either Panofsky or Rabbi Glenn Seigal could account for the Jews, Atuk, for the Eskimo. Jean-

Paul McEwen was coming and, all the way from Quebec City, an angry young priest, Father Anatole Forget. Seymour Bone would be there and so would Father Greg 'Touchdown' McKendrick, Derm Gabbard, and many, many more.

For years Norman Gore's annual buffet dinner had been an intellectual occasion unmatched on Toronto's cultural calendar. Invitations were as prized and hard come by for the tastemakers as a ticket to the Stanley Cup play-offs was among the hoi-poloi. Then, from one year to the next, the annual occasion suffered a near eclipse.

Television was responsible.

Needless to say, it wasn't that Gore's guests were the mindless sort who sat stupefied before their sets night after night. On the contrary. They were the ones who appeared on most of the programmes and that, as a matter of fact, was where the trouble lay. For traditionally it was the wittiest, the most charming, successful and intellectually formidable people who came to dine at the Gores. With the coming of television they found themselves in demand. From one week to the next, it seemed, small social graces were transformed into large earning potential. Lucy Trueman's ability to put strangers at ease and Derm Gabbard's capacity for being the life of the party both became marketable commodities. If you enjoyed having them in *your* living-room it followed that Canada, so to speak, wanted them in its national living-room. So for behaving only a little larger than they had all their lives, without thought of financial return, Lucy Trueman and Derm Gabbard were suddenly offered fabulous fees. Similarly, the man who was traditionally the most outspoken at Gore's dinners signed a whacking contract to be daring on a national network. And the story was the same with the rudest, the most handsome, and the funniest. Why even the best-read, Terry Stewart, was now a feared literary critic, and could no longer read a book unless he was paid for it.

To be fair to Gore's guests they did not cut him off completely with the advent of television. A loyal bunch, they continued to come to the house, but with one crucial difference: nobody's conversation sparkled unless he happened to be seated next to a producer. The wittiest tabletalk in Toronto was reduced, overnight as it were, to a tense exchange of monosyllables. Bone, for instance, had signed a contract promising to be offensive on *Crossed Swords* exclusively. And the truth was that bouncy, smiling Derm Gabbard was bad-tempered after a day of spreading joy through the land professionally and Lucy Trueman avoided strangers on a closed circuit. You simply couldn't expect Terry Stewart to tell you what he thought of a book for nothing. Father Greg 'Touchdown' McKendrick and Rabbi Glenn Seigal, a delightful, stimulating team in former years, did not see the point in bantering amiably about God and Man without benefit of a sponsor or a studio audience. And nobody, needless to say, would answer a question put to them by Jean-Paul McEwen unless she promised to publish the reply in full.

'They just don't act natural any more,' Gore said to his wife.

'Mm. I think it's that they're too inhibited or nervous to talk in a private room now,' Nancy said. 'A sort of inverted stage fright.'

That's when Norman Gore got his remarkable idea.

'I've got it. Why don't we put our dinners on TV?'

It was a stroke of genius. The cameras zooming in and out not only relaxed the guests, but an invitation to Gore's became an even more enviable thing: everybody collected a fee.

Each year Gore hit on a pertinent theme for his dinner. One year, as his guests were all drawn from the artistic and intellectual life, that is to say they were the most thoughtful and socially concerned citizens in Toronto, the theme was 'How to Withstand Commercialism in our Society'. (This, it must be said, proved to be such a stimulating ninety minutes that there were two summer re-runs of the show followed by a paperback publication by Mc-Farlane & Renfrew.) Another year the group turned to the theme of the Dying Art of Conversation and the Deadening Effect of TV. (Harry Snipes had some slashing comments to make about US-imported

Westerns.) But this year Professor Gore decided to open the floor to, well, just plain good talk. The dinner was without a predetermined theme.

Dinner with the Tastemakers was presented by the CBC's cultural showcase, *Fiesta*.

Though the CBC had not once come back to Gore about ratings, the Professor was somewhat anxious about this year's production. Last year he had been knocked by both *Variety* and the *Toronto University Quarterly*.

Gore sat down to a long-awaited pleasure, Panofsky's thesis. He hoped that reading it would calm his nerves. But if he was edgy to begin with, Norman Gore was in a state of alarm once he had skimmed through the manuscript.

Panofsky arrived early to discuss his thesis with the Professor.

'So?' Panofsky asked.

Gore couldn't cope.

'Yes, well, no, Mr Panofsky. Actually, what I mean to say is, no, I haven't read the *entire* thesis yet, but I have read, em, re-read your preliminary argument and I'd be less than honest if I didn't say, say at once, that it has upset me enormously.

'But it was supposed to,' Panofsky said warmly.

'Be that as it may, but – well, you correct me if I'm wrong – but I take it your hypothesis runs that contrary to what we liberals have worked so very hard and selflessly to instil in the prejudiced populace for years, you believe that Jews *are* different from other people?'

'Absolutely.'

'And that in your opinion Gentiles, well Protestants, anyway, are all similar. In fact, one Protestant is so like another that their children are interchangeable.'

'Not "in my opinion". My son and I have proven the fact scientifically. Years of research have—'

'But . . .'

Gore had always looked on tubby, grey-haired Panofsky as a gentle seeker after truth and beauty, a Jew who was a living refutation of the anti-Semitic caricature. Gore had often visualized Panofsky at his chessboard or spreading crumbs in the snow for birds. A sweet, colourful man who was in need of Gore's protection. Like Negroes. Indeed, the Professor adored Jews and Negroes so much that he felt put out when they exhibited human traits. If a Jew cheated on his income tax, for instance, or a Negro wore flashy clothes, Gore felt personally affronted. They ought not, he thought, to do that to him and other liberals after they had tried so hard to be helpful. Last year Wharton, the Negro, such a promising and ingratiating young man, had got a freshette into trouble and now there was Panofsky and his perverse thesis. Panofsky was obviously insane, certifiable, just like Gore's Uncle Jim, and this made Gore livid. They have no right to behave like us, he thought.

But before Gore could even communicate his displeasure to Panofsky the others began to arrive. Jean-Paul McEwen, Atuk and Goldie, Jersey Joe Marchette, Father McKendrick, Snipes, Rabbi Seigal, and the next thing Gore knew they were all on camera.

The first to make trouble was Father Anatole Forget. 'I will not toast the Queen,' he said to Gore.

'But we had no intention of drinking a toast.'

Father Forget could not be deceived. He knew his Ontario. 'I refuse to drink a toast to her so-called majesty whatever your plans are,' he said.

Father Forget was French Canada's leading philosopher and aesthete. Fortunately, he was soon deep in conversation with Derm Gabbard. 'Life,' he said, speaking in English, 'she is happy and life she is sad. Art is the music of the soul.'

'Oh, oui, oui,' Gabbard said, rubbing his jaw thoughtfully.

'Art makes out of colours the picture. Even more remarkable,' he said as camera 2 dollied in for a close-up, 'it takes the prosaic tree and makes out of it paper and on this paper prints words. *Et voilà, la poésie*. And herewith, one has the poetry! Some poetry is long and some poetry is short . . .'

Gore stared at Jersey Joe Marchette, puzzled. 'Haven't we met before?' he asked.

'Certainly not.'

'Funny . . .'

'Perhaps,' Jersey Joe said sharply, 'it's that we all look alike to you.'

Gore flushed.

Atuk rubbed noses with Nancy Gore, gave her the statue, and hurried to join Goldie at the buffet.

'Hey! Easy,' Goldie said, 'the whole platter isn't for you. Like you grab a little and put it on a plate.'

Bette Dolan saw them together and began to sob. Derm Gabbard patted her gently on the back. 'What is it?' he asked.

'It's Atuk; he won't even talk to me. What can he see in that fat ugly bitch?'

'We hear a lot these days,' Harry Snipes shouted, 'about Canadian artists leaving the country for Europe or the other place, where they earn a mint for writing insulting articles about their homeland. Well, I have no time for these self-haters myself. Why do they leave in the first place? Do foreign artists settle here?'

As soon as the camera zoomed in on Snipes, he pulled a little pill bottle out of his pocket – the label clearly read Morphine – and popped a couple of tablets into his mouth.

'Take away from her the crown,' Father Forget said, 'and what have you got? A woman.'

Nancy Gore moved closer to Jersey Joe Marchette.

'Another canapé?' Nancy asked.

'Thank you,' Jersey Joe said, rubbing against her leg.

'Why lookee over there,' Nancy said, withdrawing, 'there's Ruthy Bone. I hear you clean windows for her too.'

Ruthy led Seymour Bone into a corner.

'I'm going to have a baby,' she said.

'Wonderful, wonderful,' Seymour said. 'I'll announce it soon as we're on camera.'

'Wait. There's something I must tell you about my background, my Jewish background.'

'Whatever it is, dearest,' Bone said, patting her hand, 'you know I am entirely free of prejudice.'

'You see, em, one side of my family is of, ah, Yemenite extraction.'

Bone was baffled.

'Well, Yemenites are sort of brown you see. Very brown sometimes.'

'You mean *our* baby . . . ?'

'He might turn out sort of chocolate-y. Just a chance, you know. Does that bother you?'

'Of course not,' he said, trembling, anticipating all the jokes in the office. 'Why should it?'

Harry Snipes, on camera again, held up a copy of *Ejaculations, Epiphanies, et etc*; then he leaped to Buck Twentyman's defence. 'If it was only profits that interested him,' he asked, 'then why'd he build the Stage Twentyman?'

Snipes announced that one of Twentyman's many idea-men had discovered a town in northern Manitoba that was actually called Athens. Twentyman, he said, was putting a million dollars into a proposed Athens arts festival; and Snipes would be in charge. 'This will be an all-Canadian venture,' he said. 'We're going to open with a production of *Oedipus Rex*—only we're going to do it in Western costumes. The sheriff of Thebes is gunned down at a crossroads and only a little while later a notorious gun fighter, Barney "The Kid" Oedipus, rides into town . . .'

Bette tugged at Atuk's sleeve.

'Look,' he said, 'I know you went to Twentyman. Let's just forget we ever knew each other.'

Rabbi Glenn Seigal and Father Greg 'Touchdown' McKendrick began to talk shop together. Glenn told the priest the inside story of his widely reported Wedding-on-the-Ninth-Hole. 'There was many a chuckle,' he said, 'between the arrival of the best man on a go-kart and the finalization of the union.'

Both men, it developed, were worried about Sunday movies on Channel Nine. Father McKendrick told the rabbi about an enterprising priest in Victoria who had worked out a special deal with the local shopping plaza, and how he now gave away trading stamps in the confession box. 'The return to the faith, especially among young housewives, has been heartening, very heartening.'

Professor Gore joined the two men. 'What are you two reactionaries cooking up together?' he asked with a smile.

'Don't let him worry you, Rabbi. I've known Norm here for a donkey's years. When the chips are down he stands with us. One of God's ground crew, if I ever knew one.'

'This is so exciting,' Rabbi Seigal said as the camera came nearer. 'If only the bigots of this world could see us together, chatting cosily like this.'

'Judas Priest,' Father McKendrick said, 'the Rabbi's got a point there.'

'*I beg your pardon.*'

'Wait, Rabbi,' Professor Gore called. 'Come back.' The camera dollied in on Snipes again.

'The trouble with Canadians,' he said, 'is we're too damn conventional. I'll bet if I were to do something spontaneous like, just for the sake of argument, if I were to expose myself right now you'd—'

A hastily slipped in card read:

PLEASE DO NOT ADJUST YOUR SETS
THE TROUBLE IS TEMPORARY

A menacing Jean-Paul McEwen took Atuk aside.

'I know all about you and her,' she said, pointing at Bette who was sobbing on the sofa.

'But I expect to announce my engagement shortly, J-P. I've had nothing to do with Bette for months.'

'Oh, yeah. Well you just wait until you see my column tomorrow.'

'But your column always gives me immense pleasure. Say, I have an item for you. Did you know that I'm going to be the first contestant on STICK OUT YOUR NECK?'

'Are you crazy? Do you know the rules?'

Of course Atuk couldn't tell her about his under-standing with Buck Twentyman.

'All I know is that I stand to win a million. That's good enough for me.'

Nancy Gore cornered Atuk.

'You,' she said, 'enjoy – party? Have – much – fun?'

'Much-much.'

'Go eat.' Nancy Gore led him to the tables. 'Good,' she said, rubbing her stomach. 'You eat.'

Panofsky sighed impatiently, red-eyed, rocking to and fro: his glass kept spilling over.

'But of course you're a Protestant. I could tell at once. You have the typical no-face. You know, the funny little turned-up nose and the pasty complexion and—'

'What's wrong with my complexion?' Derm Gab-bard asked, retreating a step.

'But you're not to blame. It's inherited. I put it down to generations of ignorance and bad diet. You know, it's the bread you people eat. It's the Spam and the tinned pilchards and the tartar that forms between your buck-teeth from too much boozing. White Protestant, northern species; it's written all over your face, like acne. Too much pork.' He poked Derm with his elbow. 'You know what pigs thrive on, don't you?' Panofsky laughed. 'You put me in a room full of strangers and I'll pick out the goyim for you.'

'Just what have you got against us, Mr Panofsky?'

'Look around you. Take a good look.'

'Well, em, all kinds of people are Protestants, you know. We're good and bad.'

'But these I like the best. They are in the natural goy state. Pissed.'

Derm, insulted, turned to go. Panofsky grabbed him by the arm.

'A goy, Gabbard, is for running elevators or carrying a rifle. Theirs not to reason why, etc etc. On the assembly lines they're unexcelled. Look, in some fields you can't beat them. I admit it. As hockeyists, where brawn and not brain is the rule, as agriculturalists, where a taste for manure heaps is called for, the goy is supreme. Look at them, look around you, the way they guzzle the booze. Know why? They have learned to read and cannot support the weight of it. Knowledge is not natural to the goy's condition. Life has become too complex for the goy. What does he worship? The cowboy. Out there on a horse, unwashed and crawling with fleas, eating pork-beans out of a tin, and sitting tall in the saddle is the blockhead healthy goy in his natural state. Well, I'd give it back to him, bull-pies and all. Gabbard, the most boring, mediocre man in the world is the White Protestant goy, northern species, and in Canada he has found his true habitat.'

Derm Gabbard sat down on the sofa and began to talk to Bette tenderly.

His eyes red and inflamed, Panofsky went to the bar and poured himself another drink.

Harry Snipes couldn't shake Rabbi Seigal who, it appeared, was under the impression Snipes was looking for another TV series to do. So Snipes listened, making polite noises.

'You see, my son, he could be modelled after Father Brown. Of course, I'm a man of the cloth myself, hardly a thespian, so my interest in the matter is purely sociological. Such a series you know, might destroy once and for all the stereotype of the Hebrew as a physical coward. Not, you understand, that I want it to be another violent series. I don't see Rabbi Rocky Rubin in the same light as Eliot Ness. On the contrary. His would be more . . . well, the intellectual approach to crime.'

'Ah-ha.'

'Busy as I am, I would be willing to supervise the scripts for you.'

'I see.'

'Financial considerations are hardly the issue. Good taste is, Mr Snipes. Perhaps if I were to introduce each episode, as Walter Winchell does, it might give the venture a certain tone.'

'Well, Rabbi, it sure would. But I'd like to sleep on the idea.'

'You don't sound *stimulated*.'

'Oh, I am. It's very ballsy stuff, but—'

'Among my flock, you know, there's Arnold Beal. You know, Beal Distilleries. Well, he is interested in a video prestige series and I could broach the subject with him, if you like.'

'A swell idea. Can I call you tomorrow?'

'Certainly. Oh, one further thought, my son. I've mailed myself a copy of the idea by registered letter. This is no reflection on you. But I'm an innocent in these matters—'

'Yeah, sure.'

'—and I was advised—'

'Tomorrow, Rabbi, OK?'

Ti-Lucy found Atuk at the tables, filling his plate again.

'What . . . how in the hell did you get in here?' Atuk asked.

'You must come at once, Atuk. *At once.*'

Outside, a troubled Derm Gabbard led Bette towards her car. Suddenly he was seized from behind. Panofsky knocked him down, grabbed his arm, and began to twist it.

'Hey!'

Bette sat down in the snow.

'Who destroyed the Temple?' Panofsky asked.

Derm winced as Panofsky gave his arm another twist.

'Admit it. Who sacked Jerusalem?'

'Help,' Derm shouted. 'Help!'

Bette heard the call clearly and began to undress.

'Confess,' Panofsky demanded.

'Let go!'

Panofsky kicked Derm in the ribs.

'Ouch! Bette! Help me! Oh, my God. You'll
catch the death of a cold.'

'Who sacked Jerusalem? Answer, goy-boy.'

'Oooh.'

'You killed Trotsky,' he shouted, kicking him
once more.

Atuk wrapped a handkerchief round his bleeding
hand and summoned them all into the living-room
for another count. Ti-Lucy sobbed brokenly. 'It was
Ignak,' she said, 'he broke the window and—'

'It's not Ignak I'm worried about. I was going to
send him back to the Bay tomorrow anyway. Why
did Mush-Mush go with him?'

'They took some of the Queen's pictures. You
know, the green papers.'

'Some of the orange ones too, Atuk.'

'Goddam it. Back to bed. All of you.'

14

'You must find him at once. At once,' Twentyman
said. 'I warned you the story mustn't break until
Tuesday.'

'I'll do my best, Buck.'

'Didn't I offer to fly them all the way back to the
Bay at my own expense?'

'Don't worry. I'll find them.'

'You're the one who should be worried. Not me:

Atuk agreed. But, concerned as he was, the boys' escape was not his only problem. He was late for his appointment with Rabbi Siegal.

Rabbi Seigal waited by the phone in his office. Harry Snipes had not called yet. May he burn in hell, Seigal thought.

Seigal had felt secure, the Temple executive had seemed pleased when the *Standard* had decided to run his column on a three-a-week basis, but then young Bergman, the new Rabbi at the other temple, had been signed on by the *Gazette*. Rory Peel, may his teeth rot in his mouth, had made a survey and it was discovered that the little *mamzer* had a larger readership. What the *drecks* on the executive didn't understand was that Bergman ran on the same page as *Sheilah* Graham while he was buried in the classified ads section with that latter-day *yoshka* of a *Billy* Graham. Well, if Snipes took to the idea of this series . . .

'Rabbi, I'm sorry to intrude, but there's somebody here to—'

'I told you—'

'It's Atuk. The Eskimo poet. He says it's urgent. You did give him an appointment, you know.'

Atuk told the Rabbi about his trouble with Rory Peel. He explained what he wanted to do.

'I see, my son. I see.'

Rabbi Seigal turned his back to Atuk, hard put to conceal his enthusiasm. This would be the biggest catch since Sammy Davis. Bigger, by Canadian standards.

'I don't want you to rush into this, though. Perhaps you ought to reflect for a week or two. It's a big decision, Atuk.'

'You call me Abe, Rabbi. Like Abraham, may he rest in peace. I want my name altered.'

'It's good to see you're familiar with the Old Testament, but frankly we don't go in for those style names any more. What about . . . Ashley?'

'Rabbi, I want you to know I intend to study Yiddish. I—'

'Mm, Yiddish isn't necessary. We're modern Jews here, Atuk.'

'I was going to ask you about that, Rabbi. I don't mean to be impertinent, but what is that Christmas tree I saw in the hall?'

'Inter-Faith, Atuk. This year Father McKendrick will start off the Christmas dinner at the Concrete Club with chopped liver and we—'

'But the Concrete Club doesn't admit Jews. Those bastards, they—'

'We have to learn to walk before we can run, my son. Blind anger breeds violence.'

'An eye for an eye, it is written. A tooth for a tooth.'

'Tell me, son, would you object if I were to alert the press about this wedding with Miss Panofsky?'

Atuk hesitated.

'You see, last week in Miami Rabbi Bergman

scored a hole-in-one. Well, I happen to know what Bergman's game is like. I'd hate to call him a liar, but . . . Well you probably saw his picture in all the papers and—'

'Rabbi, whatever you say. Another thing I would like you to know. We're going to keep a kosher home. No *chazer-fleisch* in our house.' Atuk looked up at the ceiling. 'If I forget thee, Jerusalem.'

'Oh, that's all right. A charming custom; charming. Will you be joining our country club?'

'I hope Rory Peel will see to my application.'

The Rabbi's secretary interrupted. 'A telephone call for you, Mr Atuk. The man says it's urgent.'

It was Rory.

'We've found Mush-Mush. Two of McEwen's operators have him. They've taken him to the *Standard* office.'

On the fifth floor of the *Standard*, outside Jean-Paul McEwen's office, the two men held Mush-Mush between them on the bench. He seemed amused. He stared at the enormous redhead behind the desk at the head of the room.

The big redhead went to his filing cabinet, opened the T-Z drawer, and began to flip through some folders. T-Ty-Tyn. He found the folders he wanted, extracted a long clipping from it, and set it down beside his typewriter. 'In my estimation,' Seymour Bone wrote, 'last night's production of *The Hostage*—' Bone leaned over to study the clippings again. He frowned. 'Larry,' he called, 'be a good fellow and get me the *Shorter Oxford*, please.'

Jean-Paul McEwen opened the door. 'OK,' she said, 'bring him in. Christ, couldn't you have given him a shower first?'

'But we just took him to the can. He's afraid of water, Jean-Paul.'

'OK. Shoot.' McEwen leaned back in her swivel chair, her half-closed eyes sheltered by her hand.

'Well,' Arnold said, 'he's wandering through Loblaw's, the big one on St Clair, like in a daze, when he suddenly comes to the frozen food counter. He sees all this fish, and the next thing he's ripping packages open right there, and it takes five guys . . .'

They went on to tell McEwen how the little fellow, who said he was an Eskimo, claimed to have been separated from his brother in a crowd. The cops couldn't make anything out of his story, but they figured McEwen might be interested.

'Who figured?' McEwen demanded. 'Just who passed him on to you?'

'Captain Whitaker.'

'How many times have I told you I will accept compromising favours from no man?'

McEwen, unlike many another Toronto columnist, not only returned all cases of liquor, cheques, and automobiles, but she had also, according to report, refused birthday gifts from her nieces on the grounds that, as girl guides, they represented a pressure group.

'But wait till you hear his story, Jean-Paul. He's from Baffin Bay. He says he's been incarcerated for the last few months in a factory that makes Eskimo sculpture. He also says he can give you something hot on the DEW-line case.'

'You stupid bastards,' McEwen said, 'you know Twentyman's out to get me ever since I wrote that column on *Metro*. Well, some of his boys have put this creep on to me. He's a plant. I'm supposed to fall for his story and look like an idiot when the *Gazette* exposes me tomorrow morning. Eskimo. Look at him.'

'I'm Eskimo.'

'Charlie Chan's Number One Son,' McEwen said, 'get the hell out of my office.'

'Don't you even want to hear his DEW-line story?'

'No.'

The boys looked hurt.

'OK, OK, but make it quick.'

'Oh, one thing, Jean-Paul. He won't talk unless you show him a trick or two. You see, we've already got his confidence, to some extent.' Arnold winked. 'We showed him the magic.'

'What?'

Arnold whispered an explanation in McEwen's ear.

'Take this kook back to the funny-farm and I'll deal with you later.'

In his eagerness to reach McEwen's office the book reviewer slipped and almost fell on a banana peel as he passed the desk outside. 'Hey,' he shouted, 'wait till you hear what's happened in the john!'

'I thought that son-of-a-bitch promised to cut that out. If we lose one more copy boy—'

'No, no, it's not that again. Somebody's been in there wiping his ass with fifty-dollar bills. The floor's covered with them.'

McEwen turned on Mush-Mush. 'Empty his pockets,' she said.

Out came a few more fifty dollar bills.

'Bring me coffee. OK, fella. From the beginning. Take it nice and easy.'

'In Baffin Bay, at the time of the great ice-sheet, when the land was ours from sea to sea, was very long night—'

'Hiya!'

'Atuk!' Mush-Mush stepped quickly behind Arnold. He began to whimper.

'Hiya, J-P. I was in the neighbourhood and thought I'd drop in to tell you what a charge I got out of your column yesterday.'

'This,' Jean-Paul said, 'is beginning to get very interesting.'

Atuk picked up a fifty-dollar bill and turned to Mush-Mush; his smile magnanimous. 'There was no need to run away, kid, just because you' – he winked at Jean-Paul – 'borrowed some money. Come on, I'll buy you an ice-cream and we'll go home.'

'I no go.'

'Kid, I—'

'Ignak spoke the truth and you only lies. It is safe on the outside.'

Atuk laughed and slapped his knees. 'He kills me. Of course it's safe on the outside.'

'You frighten me no more, brother. I'm going to tell this white woman everything.'

'Sure, kid. Go ahead.'

'You mean, you don't mind?'

'You know how much I love you, Mush-Mush. Go ahead. Tell her.' Atuk grinned at Jean-Paul. 'Mind if I sit down?'

'Not at all.'

'I'm so glad the kid's safe.' Atuk jerked his head toward Mush-Mush and tapped his forehead. 'He doesn't mean any harm, you know.'

'I begin with the true DEW-line story,' Mush-Mush said ominously.

'Oh, one thing. Before you begin. Are you *sure* she's white?'

Mush-Mush drew back.

'You've had the proof?'

'Not yet.'

'Maybe you're the one who's nutty,' Jean-Paul said.

Mush-Mush whispered something to Arnold.

'Gee, I dunno,' Arnold said nervously. 'I'm not sure.'

'What is it?' Jean-Paul asked.

'He, well, like he wants you to – he wants to see your stomach exposed.'

140

McEwen looked baffled.

'You see,' Atuk said, 'my little brother feels he can't trust you, he can't be sure you're powerful white woman, until he sees your stomach. What harm can it do?'

McEwen pulled up her blouse and Mush-Mush walked around her several times. 'Give her the white pill now,' he said.

Atuk dug into his pocket. 'He wants you to take an aspirin,' he said.

McEwen took the pill, washing it down with a glass of water. Breathing quickly, Mush-Mush went round and round her. Arnold watched, alarmed. The Eskimo's smile lapsed and he looked exceedingly mean. Without warning, he seized McEwen's head and examined it closely.

'Ouch,' McEwen said, breaking free.

Mush-Mush peered intently at McEwen's chest and stomach.

'OK,' McEwen said, pulling down her blouse, 'the story. Give.'

'No. Because you are a fake. Unless—' He grabbed the pill bottle. 'Read the craziness upon it for me. Does it say X brand or—'

Atuk held up the bottle for Arnold to look at.

'Aspirin.'

'If you don't mind,' Atuk said, gathering up the fifty-dollar bills on the desk, 'I'll take my little brother home now.'

'The sooner the better,' McEwen said, still holding her head.

Atuk led Mush-Mush to the elevator. Arms raised heavenwards, eyes rolling, he said, 'Oh, descend, descend wondrous box, to street level.'

'All you have to do is press the button.'

'Know-it-all.'

'What are you going to do with me?'

'Make you a partner in the business. What else?'

'Aren't you angry?'

'You're family, Mush-Mush. How can I be angry?'

Mush-Mush told him that Ignak had returned to the Bay.

'Good.'

'You mean you will truly share profits with me?'

'Sure, kid. Now you go home and see how the others are making out.'

Mush-Mush looked left, he looked right. The rush hour traffic was at its height. 'Alone?' he asked.

'But there's no danger on the outside. You said so yourself.'

Mush-Mush began to tremble.

'It's straight ahead. You can't miss the house.' Clapping him on the shoulder, Atuk added, 'Partner.'

'OK.'

'All you have to do is remember that there are traffic lights at each corner. You see that one?'

'Yes.'

'You wait until it's red and then you run like hell. It's the only safe time to cross the street, remember.'

'When it's red.'

'Good. See you at home.'

Atuk stepped into the nearest phone booth.

'Buck, relax. Ignak's gone back to the Bay and Mush-Mush was just killed in a traffic accident.'

A car skidded. Atuk winced, waiting for the impact. It came. He made the sign of the seal.

'You'll have to speak louder, Buck. People are screaming outside.'

15

Ti-Lucy brought Atuk his morning *Standard*. Like thousands of other Torontonians, Atuk turned to Jean-Paul McEwen's column first.

SICK, SICK, SICK
By *Jean-Paul McEwen*

'Somewhere in Toronto today a used car dealer is having the speedometer "adjusted" on his '58 Chevy. A charming chap with a British accent is going club-to-club selling credulous widows shares in a uranium mine. A decent fellow, somebody who never thinks of himself as a murderer, is having "one for the road" before driving home; – and two blocks away a woman who has led a blameless life, a mother of three, starts across the street – to her death.

'As you read this, a fifty-year-old man is being told he is too old for his job. Because we have enforced religious education in our schools the innocent son of agnostic parents is being mocked by his teacher and classmates for refusing to subscribe to *Bible Comics*. *In the time it took you to read that last sentence they dumped tons of coffee beans into the Gulf of Mexico while, in Cabbage Town, hundreds of families living on relief cannot afford the price of a package*. On Spadina Avenue, a little boy has just come home with a bleeding nose. "What happened?" his mother asks. "They think I'm a sissy because I won't play Switch-Blade." She washes and tends to him, she reassures the lad, he goes upstairs to practice his piano – and one day he may grow up to be another Glenn Gould.

'In his enormous home in Forest Hill, a manufacturer who was 4-F during the war, complains to his wife that domestics aren't what they used to be, while in a rooming house on Jarvis Street a broken man takes his VC out of his cardboard suitcase and starts for the pawn shop. As you read this column a baby is being born and a man is dying . . . two youngsters are swearing eternal love and a man is telling his boy that he and Mummy are no longer attracted to each other . . . a Negro student, who will one day be in the Nigerian cabinet, has been told there are no vacancies at Twentyman Towers . . . a teacher, a ridiculed spinster, has just picked up Manny Green's essay and, reading it, she realizes that the boy is not, as others in class call him, Lard-Ass or Squint-Head, but possibly another Seymour Bone. Manny, blinking behind his thick glasses, looks up at his teacher's hairy face. To him, she is beautiful. This is Toronto. Love and injustice. Criminality and kindness. This is our city. And lurking somewhere in it is one of the foulest of the human species: the despoiler of virtue.

A GRIMM FAIRY TALE

'Once upon a time there was a pretty girl who lived in a pretty town in Ontario, and she learnt to jump higher than any other girl in the whole wide world. The girl was not only a champion, she was good and brave and generous and first Toronto, then the entire nation, took her to its heart. We cherished her. Then one fine day the girl came to live in Toronto. She became a TV and film star and soon began to meet smart people at cocktail parties. All the smart women did not like her because she was young and beautiful and all the smart men wanted something from the girl.

YOU KNOW WHAT

'The girl amazed Toronto. The smart people were confounded. For the girl would not be spoiled. She remained beautiful and brave and good until – she met a depraved man, a so-called noble savage, from our own far north. The man, quick to exploit animalistic techniques, seduced the girl.

'If my tale ended here it would be like so many others, I suppose. *But it does not end here.*

'The beautiful girl, having fallen – so to speak – once, is now falling for others as well. She thinks she is helping those other men!

'The girl is no longer pretty and her language has become . . . salty.

'This is one of the saddest tales even this world-hardened reporter has ever had to write because, like Canadians everywhere, I believed in the girl. I loved her.

'Now I know there is a name for him . . . and a name for her.

'Let's not pull punches.

'F—— and W——'

Atuk shrugged and turned to Seymour Bone's column. Today Bone had turned his discerning eye to matters other than theatrical. He was, like citizens everywhere, concerned about Strontium-90. Not only, he wrote, has it been responsible for the birth of malformed babies, but, more recently, children were being born freakishly coloured. Last month, in Alberta, an unquestionably Anglo-Saxon couple had given birth to a coloured child. It could, he warned, happen in Toronto next. Bone blamed American nuclear tests.

16

BZZZ . . ZZ . . ZZZZZ . . zz . . z . . . z . . .

Damn him, Michele Peel thought, ever since the shelter at the bottom of the garden had been finished Rory was forever at the buzzer, calling drills. Damn; but all the same she quickly hitched up her skirt, flushed the toilet, and ran.

BZZZZ . . . zzzzz . . . zzzz . . zz . . . z . . .

Atuk was subjected to a two-hour interview by network executives, producers, and advisers from the agency.

'Whatever you do,' the producer said, 'don't get a haircut between now and the show.' He measured Atuk's neck with a tape. 'Oh, would you sign these release forms, please?'

Atuk began to read. He swore he hadn't been coached, he absolved the company of all responsibilities, and then, just for form's sake, he inquired indignantly, 'Why must you have the address of my next of kin?'

'Aw, don't bother your head about it,' Derm said, clapping him on the back. 'It's just the usual legal mumbo-jumbo.'

So Atuk signed.

'That's my baby,' Derm Gabbard said.

Twentyman came round the table closer to Snipes.

'Have you read it from start to finish?' he asked.

Snipes nodded.

'You've digested all the details? I must be sure of that.'

'Sure have. It's crazy, crazy. Poor Atuk. This will be the end of him.'

Twentyman laughed. 'You've still got a lot to learn, my boy. This is only the beginning for Atuk.'

'But are you sure,' he asked, indicating the report, 'that all this is true?'

'You saw the photographs, didn't you? Do they look faked?' He didn't wait for a reply. 'Now I can assure you the details won't be released until the day after tomorrow.'

Snipes smiled.

'Don't worry. It cost me a pretty penny, but it was well worth it. Now we have plenty to do, haven't we, my boy? First there's the True Sons of Canada. I'll leave that to you. And—'

'We're ready to go with a special edition of *Metro*. As for the pickets, sir, well . . .'

Life sure does play tricks on a man. What are we to the Fates, Jock thought, but bits of sand to be blown about at will. Jock had, in all his dreams of glory won with the force, never seen himself elected Miss Canada. But there he was, waving for the cameras, throwing kisses, as he was held aloft by Niagara Fruit Belt Jr. and the Best Developed

Biceps of Sunnyside Beach. Jock was puzzled to see one of the judges, Jean-Paul McEwen, unaccountably, break down and weep. He blew her a kiss too.

Nurse Tomkins, at the Protestant Temperance Hospital, twisted her handkerchief in her hands and bit back the tears.

'Just what do you mean "Dr Zale" left instructions?' Superintendent MacKintosh demanded.

'Dr Zale. You know, the sweet old man with the assistant. The big strapping fellow.'

'Assistant! How big?' Superintendent MacKintosh asked, tapping her foot. 'Oh, six foot six at least.'

'I *see*.'

Panofsky pushed Leo inside. He kicked him.

'What is it now?' Goldie asked.

Without waiting to take off his surgical coat, Panofsky climbed on to a chair and began to pound his son over the head. 'All these years of working with me at the hospital,' he said, 'and still a butter-fingers.'

Leo tried to protect himself.

'Are we ever in for it now.'

'You're in for it anyway, Dr Kildare,' Goldie said. 'The fuzz were around asking for you this morning.'

'It doesn't matter,' Panofsky said, climbing down from the chair, 'my work is done now. They can arrest me, if they like.'

Rory Peel threw his arms up in the air, exasperated. 'Fellas, fellas,' he said, 'he's no ordinary Eskimo. Atuk would be an asset to our club.'

'For the last time,' Bernstein said, 'we're not prejudiced here. His being an Eskimo has nothing to do with it one way or another. It's that he's a goy.'

'But—'

'Rory, look at it this way. Personally, I have nothing against the goys. But if you let even a few of them in the next thing you know their kids and our kids are playing together at the pool. They go out on a date. What's one date, you say? Yeah, sure. *Then one night your daughter comes home and she wants to marry one.*'

On that fateful afternoon, when Atuk came to call, the Peel residence was charged with activity.

Michele was in the sitting-room painting a picture – an assignment from her instructor at the Temple. Setting her brush down delicately, she started for the toilet. She had only been there an instant when ... BZZZZ ... zzzz .. zzz .. z .. z ...

Neil and Garth leaped to their feet, so did Valerie, as at precisely 13.08 hours Rory pressed the button concealed under his desk top. Together the family scampered down the stairs, across the garden, and into the shelter. Rory waited grimly by the entrance. Once they were all safely inside he flicked the stop watch. 'Not bad today,' he said. '47.2 seconds off.'

Michele nodded gratefully, clutching her stomach.

'However,' Rory added severely, 'I think we can knock another thirty seconds off this time. All right! Garth!'

Quickly, the youngster secured the hatch.

'Neil!'

Rory's first-born son leaped up to man the machine gun.

'Valerie!'

The sound-effects tape was turned on and this time, Rory noted with pleasure, Garth did not weep hysterically when the bombs fell and the burning people and animals outside began to scream.

'Is it all right,' Michele asked, 'if I use the toil—'

'OK, Brunhilde,' Rory shouted through the mouthpiece to the maid waiting outside, 'zero in.'

Brunhilde forced open the hatch and towered over the family, her expression fierce.

'She forgot the ketchup,' Garth complained.

But Rory was too absorbed to comment. He paced up and down. 'OK,' he said, 'it's H-Day plus three. We're out of ammo. They've forced open the hatch. It's Mrs Springhorn from next door. Jimmy's mother.'

Neil, Valerie, and Garth waited tensely, not knowing who would get the call. Brunhilde crossed her eyes, she began to gurgle. Rory raised his arm, looked directly at Neil, and then, with a terrible suddenness, pointed the finger of command at Valerie. 'Go,' he said.

Valerie kicked the intruder in the stomach.

'Ooooh,' Brunhilde moaned.

'Quick!'

Garth charged the maid with a make-believe bayonet.

'Good boy.'

The hatch was secured.

'Rory, I'm going to burst. I simply must go to the—'

'Valerie, you can stop kicking her now. Valerie, will you please stop.'

'Thank you,' Brunhilde said.

'OK. We will assemble in the sitting-room at 14.30 hours for notes. Family dismissed.'

Atuk arrived only a short while later.

'I don't mind telling you,' Rory said, pouring him another drink, 'that I was deeply upset by our talk at the Roof Garden. That's why I didn't come into the office all week.'

'Old prejudices die hard.'

'But I've talked the whole matter over with Rabbi Seigal, you know, and I'm very proud now. I think Goldie has chosen wisely.'

'God willing, I'll do my best to make her happy.'

The doorbell rang and Rory signalled over the intercom for Brunhilde to open the door. 'That would be young Jimmy Springhorn for Valerie,' he said.

Four tall men stepped into the room. Two were in uniform. RCMP. The FBI men were in plain clothes.

'Are you Atuk, the Eskimo?'

Atuk nodded shyly.

'You're under arrest.'

An alert FBI man stepped between Atuk and the window. The Eskimo approached Rory. 'Please note,' he said quickly, 'that there are no bruises about my face and body.'

'It is my duty to inform you that anything you may say might be used against you.'

'Is much strange,' Atuk said. 'Me simple Eskimo.'

'What's the charge?' Rory asked.

'I wouldn't know . . . well, just how to put it into words.'

Part 3 This Was the Noblest Canadian of Them All

1

Legends about Buck Twentyman abounded.

Take Twentyman's student days, for instance. Even though he had inherited untold millions, young Buck had insisted on working his way through college just like less fortunate fellows. And even this early in his career, he proved himself an astonishingly resourceful man. One summer, the story goes, Buck and some other high-spirited students were hired to escort several hundred Chinese back to the west coast, from where they would embark for their homeland. For now that the Chinese had built the railroad that linked the dominion from coast to coast it was decided that they should all be repatriated. Buck was in charge of one car-load, some two hundred and ninety head, and every night he had to count his Chinese. One night, in Calgary, he and the other fellows tied one on, so to speak, and when they returned to the train Buck, taking the count, discovered he was short one head. He did not panic. He returned to town with some friends, stopped at the first laundry, found the proprietor, one Chung Lee, at dinner with his family, and kidnapped him.

Twentyman was a fearless gambler. Where other tycoons had been held back by caution Twentyman leaped ahead, always willing to back his hunches. A case in point was the new Twentyman TV Towers. When commercial, that is free enterprise, television came to Canada at last, innumerable groups bid for the Toronto franchise. But Twentyman was not downcast when other combines, considered to be more experienced and responsible by the non-Twentyman press, competed with him for a government charter. 'I relish rugged, no-holds-barred competition,' he told reporters.

Twentyman's was a sticky wicket. He had to offer the royal commission something truly Canadian, but viewers, on their side, would demand an entertaining programme schedule. Hitherto no entrepreneur had been able to combine these two seemingly incompatible elements. But Twentyman, characteristically intrepid, forged ahead. He assured the sceptics on his board that he would come up with a formula neither dull and highbrow, like the CBC, nor moronic, like the American.

The demands of the royal commission were rigorous. All bidders for the major Toronto franchise had to guarantee a schedule that was at least forty per cent Canadian in origin. Twentyman delighted them by freely promising a schedule with fifty per cent Canadian cultural content. Prominent among his indigenous offerings were Canada Hit Parade With the Three Gassers of Galt & a Girl (all Canadian-born), Trans-Canada Amateur Drama Night, a national ping-pong competition, Wednesday Wrestling, and Championship Bowling.

The board, not to say the fellows from the agency, were disheartened.

'We do not mean to sound negative, Mr Twentyman, but this package lacks zip.'

'You don't understand,' Twentyman said. 'All these admirable programmes, as well as selected National Film Board shorts, will comprise our Early, Early Show. They will be shown from five to eight each morning.'

Twentyman went on to tell them how Canadian-born Raymond Burr would appear in *Perry Mason* once a week, and that, furthermore, he had an idea for an original new show: STICK OUT YOUR NECK. Of the latter, the board commented, 'Fantastic!'

'It has everything, Buck.'

'We ought to sweep the board with it.'

Naturally Twentyman won the franchise, and only a few short weeks later he was able to begin operations.

The truth was Buck Twentyman was a fabulously lucky man.

Chung Lee, the Chinese he had kidnapped in Calgary, returned to his homeland and quickly acquired a reputation as a vehement anti-Westerner. Years later he rose to high office in the board of trade of the People's Republic. He did not forget that but for Buck Twentyman he might have ended his days in a steamy laundry on the Canadian tundra. So the first person he asked for on his return to Canada on an official visit was his erstwhile benefactor: Buck Twentyman. Professor Norman Gore, president of the Canadian-Chinese Friendship Society, was scandalized. 'But Twentyman is the worst reactionary.' Chung Lee waved his objections aside. 'Take me to Twentyman immediately,' he said.

Buck received him grandly.

'We need tractors,' Chung Lee told him.

'But the American government won't let us export them to your country.'

'We need hundreds of thousands of tractors,' Chung Lee said, 'and we are willing to pay cash on the table. I leave everything to you, Buck.'

The next day Twentyman summoned the directors of his newspapers, magazines, and radio and television stations to a meeting. 'Can you give me one good reason,' he asked, 'why each country shouldn't choose its own path to progress?'

Nobody spoke.

'Who are we to judge China?' Twentyman asked.

The directors of the Twentyman communications empire, liberals to the core, were glad of an opportunity to push a cause they believed in, and set to work merrily.

But Twentyman was still in need of a figurehead. He found him in Atuk. And today he summoned his directors and editors to an even more important meeting.

'Mm. Yes,' Twentyman said. 'He was taken into custody earlier this afternoon.'

As a murmur rose among the group Twentyman waved an arm impatiently. 'I assure you everything is under control,' he said.

'But can we count on Snipes?'

'He will serve our purpose admirably,' Twentyman said. 'About Atuk now. I—'

Everyone began to speak at once in troubled voices.

'We know what you have in mind. But power might go to the Eskimo's head.'

'He'd have us all in his grasp.'

'The dangers are—'

'—can assure you, as I said earlier, that everything will work out for the best.' Twentyman smiled one of his rare cunning smiles. 'Our cause is not in need of a hero, you know.'

'Heroes are dangerous.'

'Quite. What we need is a martyr,' Twentyman said, 'and we shall have one.'

2

Sunny Jim Woodcock, The People's Prayer for
Mayor, greeted the demonstrators on the steps of
City Hall. 'Friends,' he said, 'your cause is just, my
heart is with you, but we must not act hastily.
Violence—'

Harry Snipes stepped in front of the portly
Mayor.

'Are you lily-livered,' Snipes demanded, 'or iron-
souled? Are we men or mice?'

The answer came back in a roar.

'Good,' Snipes said, 'because I'm here to appeal
to the men among you. The weirdies and the
beardies and the queers can go home right now. As
for the rest of you . . .'

Sgt Jock Wilson slipped into his dressing gown and
went to the window to watch the people pass below.
Four men held a banner aloft that read:

FREE ATUK NOW!

Jean-Paul McEwen shouldered through the marchers
to the *Standard* offices on the other side of the street.
Somebody had heaved a rock through the window
where the crossed flags of Canada and the United
States had used to hang. Two boys tore up a sign
that read UNCLE SAM'S SAWBUCKS ACCEPTED

AT PAR and threw it into the fire. Four housewives marched toward her holding high a placard that read:

VEGETARIAN MOTHERS
DEMAND BAN
ON AMERICAN GOODS

A little further down the street an overturned car was in flames.

Norman Gore was in an extremely excited state.

'Isn't it stupendous, Nancy? I had thought our youth was dead. I didn't think anything could rouse them. It's wonderful, simply glorious. The response to Atuk's – Well, it takes me back. Not since Sacco and Vanzetti do I remember such a tremendous . . .'

Gore, who had been one of those posted to the all-night vigil outside the American Embassy, still wore his parka and ski boots.

'No. You can't sell Canada short. Why, there's more spirit to this country than . . .

BZZZZ . . . zzzzz . . . zzzz . . z . . . z . . .

McEwen strutted up and down, dictating her column.

'To begin with,' she said, 'I'd like to point out that I abhor everything American as much as the next, ah, man. The record speaks for itself. But we are going too far with Atuk. If he is guilty, and I have a witness to prove he is, then he must pay.'

The managing editor rushed into her office. 'Jean-Paul,' he said, 'I've backed you time and again, but we can't come out against Atuk. The whole country's aroused. Everybody's on his side. It would be suicide to—'

'If he's guilty he has to pay.'

Twentyman stood by the window, exultant. Below, the aroused populace marched toward the jailhouse. Their determined singing rattled the windowpane. Goldie, leading the procession, sang:

> *It's a long way to the jailhouse,*
> *it's a long way to go,*
> *it's a long way to the jailhouse,*
> *to the sweetest guy I know.*

Above, an aeroplane wrote in the sky, ATUK, WE'RE COMING.

An item at the bottom of page eight caught Norman Gore's eye.

BABY SWITCHERS
APPREHENDED

'Two men, believed to be father and son, were caught redhanded earlier today switching babies' identification bracelets in the maternity ward of the Protestant Temperance Hospital.

'The maniacs wore white jackets and surgical masks and were taken, at first, for doctors.

"I've seen them both so often over the years," Nurse Tomkins said, "that I thought they were on night staff."

'Others in the ward also recognized the two men and believed them to be Drs Zale and Shub.

'An investigation has been promised. Reached at his country home, Dr Ross McClure, President, Ontario Medical Association, said, "I can't speak until I see the full report that is being prepared. But if you think this is chaos, wait until they bring in socialized medicine."

'Meanwhile, all parents who had babies at the Protestant Temperance Hospital within the last eighteen years are urgently advised to contact Superintendent MacKintosh. "Some awkward mistakes may have been made," she said.

'The two men, when questioned, claimed to be engaged in scientific research.

'Dr F. G. Laughton, psychiatrist, has made a preliminary examination. All he would venture at this point, however, was, "The mind is the last undiscovered continent." '

'48.9 seconds today,' Rory said. 'Not very good.'

The hatch was secured again and Brunhilde lay groaning on the floor of the shelter as Garth kicked her again and again.

'Now,' Neil said, clutching his mother, 'let's play if Daddy's radioactive and I have to shoot him.'

The end. It had been, in the truest sense, Jock's dark night of the soul; and first thing the next morning he took action.

'Do you realize, sir,' he told Col Smith-Williams, 'that I am now Miss Canada?'

'Splendid, darling.'

'It's no joke.'

'But I'm not joking. We intend to use you in our new recruiting drive.'

'I have, well, I have something even more dreadful to tell you.'

For Jock, agonizing all through the night, torn between love and duty, had made the only honourable choice possible.

'I've fallen in love with a . . . man. A lad, sir.'

'Certainly, certainly. Only your private pleasures do not concern us here.'

'I have reason to believe this lad is a communist student organizer.'

'What? Why you deceitful bitch. You—'

'Wait. I intend to hand him over to you and resign from the force immediately afterwards.'

And that's how come that at seventeen thirty hours that very same evening when Jock, as usual, went to meet Jim in the park, the surrounding area was charged with cunning activity. The two plump, seemingly innocent nurses gossiping at the end of the footpath were actually the cleverest of commandos; the prams they rocked were stuffed with hand grenades and tear gas bombs. A helicopter hovered overhead. The happy little boy and his dog wrestling on the grass were not what they appeared to be either. The boy was the only midget in the RCMP and the dog, of course, was a trained killer. Furthermore, the old rabbi, ostensibly snoozing two benches away, actually clutched a machine gun under his kaftan. In the car parked on the street alongside – a vehicle equipped with the most foolproof of radar devices – Col Smith-Williams checked to see if all systems were go just as Jock, stunning in the black Balenciaga he had chosen for the occasion, sat down on the bench to wait. But at the appointed hour it was not Jim who came striding purposefully down the path but Jean-Paul McEwen, for she too had chosen this evening to reveal all. Jean-Paul wore a silk blouse, tweed skirt, and sensible shoes.

'Jane,' Jean-Paul said.

'Go away,' Jock said, 'I'm waiting for—'

Jean-Paul, her eyes moist, lit a Schimmelpenninck.

'Good God, it's you!'

'Yes, my poor darling, it's me.'

'You're not a lad then. You're a woman.'

'Like you.'

Jock ripped off his wig triumphantly. 'No. Not like me. For you see I'm a man,' he said, rubberized breasts heaving.

The lovers embraced and quickly explained all to

Col Smith-Williams and his men who had moved in on the couple, guns drawn.

'Jock.'

'Jean-Paul.'

'So I'm not a queer.'

'No. And I'm not a dyke,' Jean-Paul said, pulling Jock onto her lap.

'All right. Enough of the mushy stuff,' Col Smith-Williams said, disgruntled. 'Get that wig back on before anyone sees you. That's an order, Sergeant. There's still the Miss Universe contest ahead of us.'

3

Once Colonel Swiggert's bones were discovered and it was established, beyond a doubt, that Atuk had eaten him, the Americans expected swift justice. Misinformed, as usual, they had not figured on the fresh spirit of nationalism that was rampant in the dominion. As for Atuk, it was reported that his only request was that his little brothers and sisters should be allowed to return safely to their natural habitat – the Bay he would see no more.

The afternoon of Atuk's arrest the country – stunned – maybe even a little astonished by the nature of the Eskimo poet's crime – was still. The giant of the north held its breath. Knocked back on its heels, Canada needed time. Fortunately, not that much time. For only a half hour after Atuk was incarcerated a series of man-on-the-street interviews carried by the CBC revealed that plain people everywhere were heart and soul with the Eskimo.

'He has such a nice face,' a Saskatoon housewife said. While a hospital dietician in Victoria said, 'He must have been *very* hungry.' A man in Calgary asked, 'What was that Yankee blankety-blank doing in our arctic, anyway?' Another, in Moncton, said, 'Where were they in 1916 or '39. Ask 'em that.'

One by one the people were heard.

'Johnny Canuck,' a CBC commentator said, shedding his horn-rimmed glasses and looking very severe, 'has been roused from his slumber. From coast to coast he speaks. The accents differ, but the voice is the same.' Frowning deeply, he put on his glasses again. 'The voice,' he said, 'is an angry one.'

The Canadians spoke up.

A mechanic who had been fired by General Motors; a man whose Buick had broken down and another with a GE mix-master that didn't work; a widow who had bought oil shares in a Texas swamp; another whose most unforgettable character had been rejected by the *Reader's Digest*; a couple who had been asked for their marriage licence in a Florida motel; a retired army officer who, presenting a twenty-dollar bill in a New York restaurant, had been asked, 'What's this, baby? Monopoly money . . .'; people who didn't like last week's Ed Sullivan show or felt they ought to give Toronto a major league baseball team; some who recalled

Senator McCarthy; a man whose claim against All-State hadn't been honoured; a politician who had never made the Canadian section of *Time*; and more, many more, wrote to their newspapers, phoned their local television stations, and wired their MPs.

Only a hop, skip, and a jump behind came the intellectuals.

'What sort of example,' Seymour Bone demanded, 'has, say, Charles Van Doren set for a simple Eskimo?'

A prominent sports writer recalled the Chicago baseball scandal.

'This is not a banana republic,' an important novelist said.

A University of Toronto psychologist pointed out, 'Atuk's act was one of symbolic revenge. Culturally, economically, the Americans are eating our whole country alive.'

'The poet,' a western critic said, 'is essentially a childish person. You can't apply normal standards of behaviour to the creative ones. Really, there's no saying what they'll do next.'

'Like they killed Dylan,' Harry Snipes said.

During the night American cars were wrecked by wandering hordes, Coca-Cola signs were ripped down, and copies of American books were burned on street corners. The CBC hastily cancelled a production of *Our Town*.

Alert producers dug into bottom drawers and hurried from place to place with pilot films for series to replace *Wagon Train*, *The Defenders*, and *Ben Casey*. Jimmy McFarlane of McFarlane & Renfrew ordered an immediate reprint of *Eskimo Song*, proceeds for the Atuk Defence Fund. By morning the fat was in the fire.

'While we would be the last to condone cannibalism,' the editorial writer on the *Standard* wrote, 'we do feel that Atuk, a simple man, is a special case. US Army officers had no business in his land disturbing an age-old and time-honoured way of life. Flatly, pardon him. We're passing the buck to you, Dief.'

The *Post* was even more forceful.

'One of the most neglected, long-suffering, and tragic of our minority groups has suffered another blow to its pride. The noble Eskimo never complains. For help he asks us not. Freedom-loving, proud, he asks only to be allowed to hunt as his father's fathers have before him. Unlike other minority groups we could cite he has organized no anti-defamation leagues. He sends no representatives to make long-winded speeches at that excuse for a debating club, the UN. Yet who is more entitled to aid than the original Canadian? What ethnic group are we more indebted to? None.

'Yet we allow armed and ignorant foreigners to enter his land and meddle with his folk practices. Practices unfathomable to us, I gainsay, but sacred to our brothers in the igloo. The question, it seems to me, is not did he eat or not eat him. I wouldn't.

You wouldn't. But live and let live has always been our policy. What the Eskimo does in his land is not our affair – and certainly not Uncle Sam's. The trouble with the affluent society to the south of us is that they have been ruined by status-seeking and hidden persuasion and dream-merchants. They would impose conformity on all of us. Take back your minks, we say. Your homosexual playwrights can stay home. We don't need your pipe-lines. But, above all, leave our Eskimos alone.'

HANDS OFF THE ESKIMO, the *Gazette* headline demanded, and, on its editorial page, it recommended a sympathy march on Ottawa. Suddenly, as if by a sweep of Twentyman's hand, march co-ordinators, group captains, bands, placards, Esky-Food trucks, and helicopter ambulances appeared in strategic areas. Snipes, of *Metro*, promised a Miss Liberation Contest. Newspapers all across Canada, from left to right, came out solidly behind Atuk, though none went so far as the communist weekly *Tribune*. IT'S A WONDER, the *Tribune* headline read, HE DIDN'T DIE OF PTO-MAINE POISONING.

Atuk, with Rabbi Glenn Seigal almost constantly by his side, made only one short, simple statement.

'Is much sadness for me here. Man against man. Ungood. Tell them back at the Bay, Atuk will try to die tall, even as the Old One taught us in happier hunting days.'

Only Jean-Paul McEwen came out fearlessly against the Eskimo. She demanded the death sentence for Atuk. But, as the *Gazette* pointed out compassionately in a later editorial, McEwen had relatives in the United States, and it was just possible that their safety had been threatened. Under a headline, NO COMMENT, the *Post* published a picture of McEwen shaking hands with an American lady senator. The columnist's effectiveness was undermined, and the concept (shortly to become an alarming actuality) of the Committee to Investigate Pro-American Activities was born.

BZZZ . . . zzzz . . . zzz . . zz . . z . . z . . .

Singing, full of fight, the marchers moved on the jailhouse.

> GOLDIE: *In the condemned cell of the jailhouse,*
> *his head hanging low,*
> *sits my love, Atuk,*
> *a-waiting to go.*

'45.8,' Rory said. 'Good.' He reached for the mouthpiece. 'All right, Brunhilde. Zero in.'

Nothing.

'Zero in, Brunhilde!'

All eyes were on the hatch. Clang! It seemed, oddly enough, like something had been jammed into place outside.

'Brunhilde, will you zero in please.'

All the senior directors of Twentyman's vast, inter-locking pyramid of food enterprises were assembled in the board room, waiting.

'Can't understand it,' Farley said. 'Rory's never been late before.'

Another director spoke up bitterly. 'I don't blame him for being late. I've never questioned Buck's judgement before,' he said, turning to the others, 'but I don't see how we're going to get Esky-Foods off the ground. Do you realize that this puts us in direct competition with one of America's largest, most deeply entrenched, go-ahead food combines?'

Nobody dared add that Twentyman, to the astonishment of all of them, had suddenly leased the rights to STICK OUT YOUR NECK to the same American combine. His arch-competitor in a new field.

'I think this time Buck has over-stepped the mark in more ways than one,' another director finally said.

'Harry's right. He's created a Frankenstein. If Atuk's pardoned, and it just looks like he might be, there's no saying what in the hell he'll do next.'

'And if he isn't the country will go hog-wild. A beast without a head.'

'But Buck can—'

'They'd never accept Buck as a leader. Let's face it, he's universally despised.'

'Buck's bitten off big pieces before and he's never gone wrong.'

'I think the trouble is he never figured on Atuk getting so much support across the country.'

'Nonsense. Buck always figures every angle.'

'Maybe, but this time, whatever happens, he's in for trouble.'

It was almost time for STICK OUT YOUR NECK. Bette was escorted to a waiting limousine.

'Easy does it.'

'But Atuk's in jail. How can he—?'

'They're letting him out under armed escort to appear on the show.'

'Well,' Bette said, 'you have to give him credit no matter what. He's certainly shooting for the bull's-eye tonight.'

Rory seized his mouthpiece again. 'Brunhilde, I know you're out there. Now listen, listen carefully. I have an important appointment in town. This joke has gone far enough. Now will you please open up?'

But it seemed to Rory he heard a car, his car, drive off.

The marchers shouted, 'We want Atuk! We want Atuk!'

Panofsky shielded his eyes from the brilliant

173

light. 'I'd like to help you, captain. But there were so many, so many names. It was all in the interest of scientific research, you know.'

Derm Gabbard skipped onstage before the cheering studio audience. 'Hiya, folks!'

'Hi, Derm!'

'Folks, it's time for . . .?'

'STICK OUT YOUR NECK!'

An electronic button was pressed, a curtain lifted, and revealed was an enormous wire tub packed with a million in one dollar bills.

'Ooooh!'

'Wow!'

Derm dived into the tubful of money, threw a shower of bills in the air, giggled, and dived again as four guards released the safety catches on their sub-machine guns and stepped closer to the audience. Derm came up again, his eyes crossed. He sang, 'It isn't raining rain, you know . . . it's raining GOLD! SILVER! DOLLARS!'

Another electronic button was pressed, another curtain rose, the Calgary Coyotes struck up 'For He's A Jolly Good Fellow', and for the first time the audience saw the contestant, Atuk, his head locked in a guillotine.

'Come on, folks,' Derm demanded, 'let's have a great big hand for Atuk.'

Everyone applauded.

'Is he a good sport?'

'*Yes.*'

'*You said it, Derm!*'

'I want you to know, folks, that this is no phoney-style American quiz show. Have you been given any hints, Atuk?'

'No, sir.'

'Have you been coached?'

'No, sir.'

Derm winked at the studio audience. 'Nervous?' he asked, grinning.

'Yes, sir.'

'You betcha. You betcha life he is! Whoops, time for the commercial.'

The message from the frozen food combine, one of the largest in the United States, had been filmed in New York.

Twentyman waved and smiled. Atuk smiled back. Above, the blade gleamed.

'Watcha going to do with all the loot, if you win?' Derm asked.

'Build a hospital for my people on the Bay.'

'Waddiya say, gang? Isn't he terrific?'

Cheers. Whistles.

'Well, folks, you all know the rules. Two warm-up questions and then *the* question and then he . . .?' Derm leaned toward the audience, cupping his ear. 'He . . .?'

'STICKS HIS NECK OUT!'

'Righty-ho! If he's right the million smackers are

his but if he's wrong . . .' Derm made a sweeping gesture. 'KER-PLUNK!'

Cameras cut to nurses and male attendants as they assumed their places among the audience. A doctor and two nurses, the latter wearing black tights and net stockings, appeared onstage. One of the nurses stooped, kissed Atuk's head, and placed a basket underneath it. The other wound a strap round his arm. Atuk winked at Goldie.

'What's his blood pressure?' Derm asked.

'High-ish.'

'You betcha life it is! Pulse?'

'The same.'

'Whoops. Time for a word or two from our sponsor. Back in a mo.'

Niagara Fruit Belt Jr and Best Developed Biceps of Sunnyside Beach stood watch in the shadows. Doc Burt Parks's instructions had been clear. Nobody on board must be allowed to molest her. And there were drunken flirts everywhere.

Jock pulled his shawl more snugly round his shoulders and looked out to sea. It was lonely, so bitterly lonely, without her. What did all those stars, the moon's enchantment, a closet full of ravishing gowns, mean to him without Jean-Paul. Who did he dress for, if not Jean-Paul. And yet, and yet, if he did win the Miss Universe contest, wouldn't she be proud? Col Smith-Williams too. Why, it would be another first for the force. An historic first.

'Okey-doke,' Derm said. 'Your category of questions Atuk, is HOCKEY!'

'*Gevalt!*'

But Twentyman smiled discreetly and gave Atuk the V for Victory sign.

'Who won the Stanley Cup last year?'

'Mm.'

'Tempus fidgets, tempus fidgets, Atuk.'

Twentyman flashed a little card in the palm of his hand.

'The Montreal Canadians?'

'Kee-rect!'

'What's the name of the first man to score fifty goals in a regular season?'

'Rocket, em, Richardson?'

'Close. Very close, but—'

Again Twentyman flashed a card.

'Richard!'

'Kee-rect. And now, Atuk, you . . .?'

'STICK OUT YOUR NECK!'

'For a million bucks, Atuk, can you tell me the total number of third period goals scored by Howie Morenz in regular season play and how many of these were slap-shots, how many rebounds, and how many were scored when the opposition was a man short . . . Atuk, STICK OUT YOUR NECK.'

Atuk turned confidently toward Twentyman, but his seat in the first row was empty. He had gone. The drums rolled, the studio clock began to tick, and a man in a black hat stood ready to draw the cord.

'There's been a mistake, sir. I—'
KER-PLUNK!
'Tough luck, Atuk, next week, folks . . .'

On the square outside the prison where the thousands stood with their torches and placards, Twentyman mounted the platform, stepped closer to Snipes, and whispered something in his ear. Snipes nodded. He approached the microphone and called for silence. Slowly the singing, the shouting, died; the crowd quietened. Snipes tugged at his baseball cap, looked scornfully into the television camera, and rubbed the beard that was just beginning to grow.

'Atuk is dead.' He told them how, where, and pointed out the country of origin of the show's sponsor. 'Friends, Canucks, countrymen,' he went on, 'use your noggins . . .'

Afterword

BY PETER GZOWSKI

A photograph on the back of the first edition of *The Incomparable Atuk* shows the author in familiar costume: white shirt, collar unbuttoned, thin tie loosened. His head is cocked, and he is gazing, with uncharacteristic earnestness, at what one takes to be an off-camera interviewer. His forearms are crossed, and his hands are out of frame, but to anyone who remembers him from those days it is almost certain that in the fingers of the right is a small smelly cigar – probably, in fact, a Schimmelpennick, which he used to buy at the Park Plaza smoke shop when he was in Toronto, and which, in *Atuk*, he puts in the hands of the columnist Jean-Paul McEwen. He looks freshly shaven, so my guess is it's morning; otherwise, I'm sure, there'd be a snifter of Remy Martin somewhere near as well.

Mordecai was thirty-two in 1963, when *Atuk* was published. He's a bit older than I and Robert Fulford, a bit younger than Ken Lefolii, who was managing editor of *Maclean's*, where Bob and I also worked, and Jack McClelland, who'd published all his books. But he's of the same time. For a while at least, he was also of the same place. All of us wore white shirts, loosened our ties, and tried to hone our craft or, in his case (for the craft of journalism, which he practised with his own sardonic skills, was a base from which to aim for a higher league), art.

In 1958, when he was living in England, he'd sold *Maclean's* a piece called "How I became an unknown with my first novel." (The four-hundred-dollar fee, he said, was more than he'd made out of *The Acrobats*.) The next year, we ran a couple of excerpts from *The Apprenticeship of Duddy Kravitz*, and later, a "For the sake of argument" (a catch-all for stuff we wanted to publish but not necessarily endorse) called "We Jews are almost as bad as the Gentiles." Somewhere around then – neither of us remembers exactly when – Mordecai and Florence and their brood moved back to Canada, splitting a year between Montreal and Toronto. He wrote regularly for us in those years, including a memoir called "Making it with the chicks" ("It had all started, it seemed to me . . . on the day I had begun to look up bad words in the Shorter Oxford Dictionary, which they kept right out in the open at the Y"), which we bought when Ralph Allen, the editor, was on holiday. "Making it" made Ralph, who was puritanical about what ran in *Maclean's*, furious. "Masturbating behind the barn," I remember him saying, though it's pretty tame if you look it up now.

Maclean's isn't *Metro*, *the magazine for cool canucks*, if that's what you're thinking. If there is a model for Harry Snipes's mag, it's *Liberty*, in which Frank Rasky, and sometimes Hugh Garner, ran articles of the sort Richler attributes to Snipes. Garner, in fact, under such pseudonyms as Jarvis Warwick, used to specialize in writing both sides of *Liberty*'s balanced pros and cons: both "A Moose Jaw housewife tells how fluoridation saved her marriage" *and* " 'Rat poison!' says a Fredericton hygienist." At the top of those and other pieces, *Liberty* used to run the "reading time." Twelve minutes or more, as I remember, was a toughie. Frank Rasky used to have himself paged in airports, too, so people would know he was in town. But Mordecai, who has always seen with his own eyes, either didn't know those things or didn't care.

With other clefs as well, it's easy to be misled. Nathan

Cohen, of course, was Toronto's pre-eminent drama critic of the time, as well as the host of *Fighting Words*, a program remarkably similar to Seymour Bone's *Crossed Swords* (it's too bad it's Dr. Burt Parks who gets to say, "I'm world famous all over Canada"). And Pierre Berton was writing his justly famous column in the *Star*, making good use of "operatives" (not operators) – most of Pierre's agents, by the way, were one remarkable housewife – as well as carrying out most of the extracurricular work Mordecai attributes to Jean-Paul McEwen. (I wonder what the author of the wonderful Jacob Two-Two books makes now of having poked fun at someone publishing the "bedtime stories she made up for her nieces.") But Nathan for all his pretensions, and he doubtless was the "Canada's rudest drama critic," made neither secret nor fuss of his Jewishness, and came from Cape Breton, not the prairies. Pierre, heaven forfend, didn't smoke – Schimmelpennicks or anything else. As for cross-dressing, are you kidding?

And so on. Others in *Atuk's* antic cast with obvious roots in reality – Jimmy McFarlane, of "McFarlane and Renfrew," Rabbi Glenn Seigal (surely Abraham Feinberg of Holy Blossom Temple), Sunny Jim Woodcock (Nathan Phillips was "Mayor of All the People") – play minor roles. They're included, I think, only because it amuses Mordecai to see them, as it amused him once to insert into a movie script a thug called "Zosky." ("What you dare to dream, dare to do," by the way, is straight out of a booklet published by Ben Weider, the Montrealer who has made himself rich and famous as a body-builder, and the subject of another Richler magazine article.) The big parts – Bette Dolan, Rory Peel, Twentyman himself (though there are touches of John Bassett there, and maybe Jack Kent Cooke) – are all either composites, fabrications, or, like Bone and McEwen, skewed away from recognizability. The characteristics that skew them, moreover, are satirically pointless – funny, of course, but harmless.

However tough the book is on Toronto of the time, in other words, and on the excesses of cultural nationalism, the personal attacks are missing; no one's hurt.

Which is, when you think of it, not surprising. Among many other qualities that might confound people who know him only by reputation, Mordecai Richler is a very nice man, a gentleman, as my grandmother would have said, old-fashioned. In person, he cares more than anyone else I know about marriage, the family, loyalty to his friends. In his non-fiction, to be sure, he is capable of writing down every stupid thing people say to him and reporting it with a scathing lack of guile. But in his fiction, like a boxer who realizes his fists are lethal weapons, he holds back, attacks the idea, not the holder. He is, dare I say it, a Canadian.

Thirty-two, eh? So much is already there. The exquisite ear, the eye for the vainglorious, the staccato rhythms, the sentences boiled down to Jesus-wept economy, and, even in this slim volume, the Dickensian richness of the *dramatis personae*. Some of the jokes in *Atuk* reach too desperately, of course, (a reindeer knuckle? smoked caribou at "Benny's?"), and some of the language ("Negroes," "ofays") rings dated, or smacks of dangerous stereotype. But even then, you can tell, Richler had found his voice.

Anti-Canadian? No, anti-*folly*. In his determination that we honour that which is excellent rather than simply that which is Canadian, Richler could be seen, in fact, as the most *pro*-Canadian of writers. "The truth is," he wrote once, "if we were indeed hemmed in by the boring, the inane, and the absurd, we foolishly blamed it all on Canada, failing to grasp that we would suffer from a surfeit of the boring, the inane, and the absurd wherever we eventually settled."

In Canada, in 1963, he put our world through the lens of his comic imagination, saw some things the rest of us didn't see, amused himself, and warned us all where we were heading.

I still wonder if we heard him.